T0022868

DAWNSHARD

BRANDON SANDERSON

DAWNSHARD

TOR

A TOM DOHERTY ASSOCIATES BOOK

NEW YORK

DAWNSHARD

Copyright © 2020 by Dragonsteel Entertainment, LLC
Illustrations copyright © 2020 by Dragonsteel Entertainment, LLC

Mistborn®, The Stormlight Archive®, Reckoners®, Cosmere®, and Brandon Sanderson® are registered trademarks of Dragonsteel Entertainment, LLC.

All rights reserved.

Illustrations by Ben McSweeney

A Tor Book
Published by Tom Doherty Associates
120 Broadway
New York, NY 10271

www.tor-forge.com

Tor® is a registered trademark of Macmillan Publishing Group, LLC.

The Library of Congress Cataloging-in-Publication Data is available upon request.

ISBN 978-1-250-85055-3 (paper over board)

Our books may be purchased in bulk for promotional, educational, or business use. Please contact your local bookseller or the Macmillan Corporate and Premium Sales Department at 1-800-221-7945, extension 5442, or by email at MacmillanSpecialMarkets@macmillan.com.

Originally published by Dragonsteel Entertainment
in November 2020

First Tor Edition: November 2021

Printed in the United States of America

0 9 8

For Kathleen Dorsey Sanderson
Who is the person I know that best deserves her own larkin. (For now, her cats will have to do.)

PROLOGUE

Nothing could compete with the experience of dangling from the rigging tens of feet in the air—fresh sea air in your face—while looking across an infinite plane of shimmering blue water. The vast ocean was an open roadway. An individual invitation to explore.

People feared the sea, but Yalb had never understood that. The sea was so open, so welcoming. Pay her a little respect, and she would carry you anywhere you wished to go. She'd even feed you along the way and lull you to sleep with her songs at night.

He took a deep, full breath—tasting the salt, watching windspren dance past—and grinned ear to ear. Yes, nothing could compare to these moments. But the chance to win a few spheres off the new guy . . . well, that *did* come close.

Dok clung to the rigging with the tight grip of a man who didn't want to fall—rather than the loose control of one who knew he wouldn't. The fellow was competent, for an Alethi. Most of them never set foot on ships except to cross particularly wide ponds. This guy, however, not only knew his port from his starboard, he could legitimately haul on a bowline and reef a sail without hanging himself.

But he held on too tightly. And he grabbed the rail when the ship swayed. And he had fallen seasick on the third day. So while Dok was *close* to being a real sailor, he wasn't quite there. And since Yalb made a point of keeping an eye on new sailors these days, it fell to him to help Dok via a good pranking. If the Alethi queen wanted more of her people trained in Thaylen sailing traditions, they'd need to learn this part too. It was educational.

"There!" Yalb said, leaning out and pointing with one hand as he swayed in the breeze. "You see it?"

"Where?" Dok climbed higher, scanning the horizon.

"Right there!" Yalb pointed again. "Big spren, emerging from the waters near where the sunlight reflects."

"No," Dok said.

"Huh. It's *right there*, Dok. Enormous sailorspren. Guess you ain't—"

"Wait!" Dok shaded his eyes. "I see it!"

"Really?" Yalb said. "What does it look like?"

"A vast yellow spren?" Dok said. "Rising out of the water? It has big tentacles, waving in the air. And . . . and a bright red stripe on its back."

"Well toss me overboard and call me a fish," Yalb said. "If you can see it, I guess you *are* a real sailor! You win the bet, then."

Of course, they'd made certain Dok could hear them whispering when they'd discussed these supposed "sailorspren," so he knew what description to give. Yalb fished a few chips from his pocket and handed them to Dok. Easy early winnings to facilitate Dok's playing along more and more. He'd see manifestations of the "sailorspren" everywhere until—after putting a huge bet on the table that he could catch one—it was revealed that there was no such thing as a sailorspren, and everyone would have a big laugh.

Way Yalb saw it, if a fellow was naive enough to get pranked, then he'd lose all his spheres *eventually*. Why not lose them to mates? Besides, they'd keep the spheres to buy everyone—Dok included—rounds on shore leave. After all, once you got your mates drunk, that was when you became a *real* sailor. Plus, once they were sloshed enough, maybe they would *all* see a bunch of bright yellow spren with tentacles.

Dok settled into the rigging. "Is it true you sank once, Yalb?"

"The ship sank," Yalb said. "I merely happened to be a resident thereon."

"Not what I heard," Dok said, his voice lightly spiced with an Alethi accent. "Didn't you tell people the whole storming ship vanished underneath you?"

"Yeah, well, I swallowed half the ocean before someone fished me out," Yalb said. "I wasn't exactly a reliable witness at that point, was I?"

And he'd find the sailor who was repeating that story, then sew his hammock shut. They knew Yalb didn't like talking about the night the *Wind's Pleasure* had gone down. It had been a good ship, with a better crew. Of them, only three had survived.

The other two told the same terrible story, same as Yalb remembered it. Assassins in the dark— something worse than a mutiny. And then . . . the whole ship just *gone*. For months he'd thought himself insane. But then the whole storming world had gone insane, with Voidbringers returning, a new storm blowing in, and everyone at war.

So now he had Alethi on his ship. And he'd keep an eye on anyone new, to be safe. Dok seemed a good sort though, so Yalb was going to treat him right—by treating him wrong.

Yalb leaned out farther, trying to recover his

mood. "Now that you've seen the sailorspren, you can . . ." He frowned. What was *that*? Marring the infinite blue beauty?

"What?" Dok asked, eager. "I can what, Yalb?"

"Hush," Yalb said, climbing up to the eel's nest to wave at Brekv, who was on duty. "Three points off the port bow!"

Brekv spun and searched that direction, raising his spyglass. Then he swore softly.

"What?" Yalb said.

"Ship. Wait a minute. It's coming up over the curve. . . . Yeah, it's a ship, sails in tatters. Listing to port. How'd you ever spot it?"

"What banner does it fly?"

"None," Brekv said, handing down the spyglass.

A bad sign. Why was it out here alone, during a war? Yalb's own vessel was a quick scouting vessel, so it made sense for them to sail alone. But a merchant ship would want an escort these days.

Yalb focused on the ship. No crew on deck. Storms. He handed the spyglass back.

"You want to report it?" Brekv asked.

Yalb nodded, then went sliding down the line past Dok, who looked on with surprise. Yalb leaped off the rope and hit the deck running, then was up to the captain's post in three jumps, skipping half the steps.

"What?" Captain Smta said. She was a tall woman, with her eyebrows in curls to match her hair.

"Ship," Yalb said. "No crew on deck. Three points off the port bow."

The captain glanced toward the helmswoman, then nodded. Orders went out to the men in the rigging. The ship turned toward the newly sighted vessel.

"You take a boarding party, Yalb," the captain said. "In case your special experience is needed."

Special experience. The rumors weren't true, but everyone believed them, whispering that Yalb had sailed on a ghost ship for years—which was why it had eventually vanished. There was a reason nobody would hire all three of the survivors together, and they'd had to go their own ways.

He didn't complain at the treatment. The captain had been good to take him. So if she ordered him, he'd do it. Indeed, though he was a mere seaman with no authority, even the first mate looked to him for orders as they finally pulled up beside the strange ship. Sails all torn to shreds. Listing in the water with a deck empty of even ghosts.

It didn't vanish beneath their feet as they explored it. An hour of searching later, they returned empty-handed. No sign of any ship's log, and no sign of any crew—living or dead. Only a name. *First*

Dreams, a private ship the first mate remembered hearing about. It had vanished five months prior during some kind of mysterious voyage.

As Yalb waited for the captain and the others to discuss what to do, he leaned against the railing and studied the unfortunate ship, drifting forlorn. Was it fate that *he* should find this vessel? That the man whose ship had vanished now joined with the ship whose crew had vanished? The captain would want to break out an extra sail and bring this one home. Yalb was certain of it. They needed every ship in the war effort.

They were going to put him on it. He knew they were. The storming queen herself would likely demand it.

The sea was a strange mistress indeed. Open. Welcoming. Inviting.

Sometimes a little too much so.

1

Some people might have considered it boring work to select a new trade expedition. To Rysn, it was a thrilling chase. Yes, she did it sitting in a room surrounded by stacks of papers, but she felt like a hunter all the same.

Among these reports hid so many interesting tidbits. Details of goods for sale, rumors of ports with needs that the war was making difficult to fulfill. Somewhere among all of this minutia was the perfect opportunity for her crew. She sorted through it like a scout creeping through the underbrush, quiet and careful, seeking the perfect line of attack.

Plus, diving into something so involved distracted her from other worries. Unfortunately, as soon as she thought that, Rysn couldn't help glancing at Chiri-Chiri. Covered in carapace, with large membranous wings, the larkin ordinarily spent her days pestering Rysn for food or otherwise getting into trouble. But today, like so many recently, the larkin was curled up, sleeping at the far end of the long table, near Rysn's pot of grass from Shinovar.

Chiri-Chiri had grown to roughly a foot long from her snout to the base of her tail—which extended another fifteen inches. She was big enough that Rysn needed two hands to carry her. The larkin cut an impressive profile, with her pointed mandibles and predator's eyes. But these days, her normally brown-violet shell had whitened to an almost chalky color. Too white—this wasn't a simple molt. Something was wrong.

Rysn slid along her bench. In the past, she'd preferred a tiny office set off from others. She now thought she'd done that unconsciously because she'd wanted to hide away.

No more of that. She now had a large office, in which she'd commissioned a variety of furniture changes. Though she'd lost the use of her legs in her accident two years ago, her injury wasn't as far up along her spine as other people she'd written to. Rysn could sit on her own, though doing so strained her muscles unless she had a backrest to lean against. Even then, she felt it was good practice to sit and strengthen her muscles.

Instead of a chair—or a series of them—she preferred long benches with high backs, which she could
slide along. She'd ordered them built along the various long tables in the office, which also had a large
number of windows. It felt so open and free now; she
found it remarkable she'd ever preferred something
much smaller and darker.

She reached the end of the bench, near Chiri-
Chiri's nest of blankets. Rysn set down her pen and
plucked a diamond sphere from the nearby gob-
let, then nudged it over to Chiri-Chiri. It glowed
brightly, inviting the larkin to feast on its Stormlight.

Chiri-Chiri only cracked a silver eye and barely
stirred. A few anxietyspren, like twisting black cross
shapes, appeared around Rysn. Storms. The animal
doctors hadn't been able to offer much aid—they
guessed she had a disease, but said that diseases were
very individualized to a species. And Chiri-Chiri
was the sole member of her species any of them had
ever seen.

Trying not to let the worry crush her, Rysn left
the sphere near Chiri-Chiri's mouth, then forced herself to return to her hunt. She'd already sent a request
via spanreed to someone she thought could help with
Chiri-Chiri. There wasn't anything more Rysn could
do until he replied. So, she scooted along her bench to

resume her work. Then, however, she realized she'd
left her pen. She began to scoot back to fetch it.

Immediately, Nikli bounded out of his position
near the doorway and scrambled to grab the pen for
her. Before she could arrive, the overeager man had
the tool proffered.

Rysn sighed. Nikli was her new head porter, the
man who carried her between locations when she
needed help. He was from somewhere in the western
Makabaki region, and though his Thaylen was good,
he'd had trouble finding work. He stood out, with
his face and arms covered in white tattoos.

He was eager to keep his job, but while she appreciated initiative . . . "Thank you, Nikli," she
said, taking the pen. "But please wait until I ask for
help before rendering it."

"Oh!" he said. He bowed. "Sorry."

"It's all right," she said, waving for him to retreat
to the side of the room. His attitude wasn't uncommon. When she'd explained the benches for her office, the initial response had been confusion. "But
why?" the carpenters' foreman had asked.

Ah, to be free of the "but why."

To everyone else, her actions seemed odd. She was
a trademaster, with her own ship and crew. She could
order servants to fetch her anything she needed. And
she did need help now and then.

The thing was, she didn't *always* need help. It was a lesson she herself had been forced to learn, so she didn't blame Nikli for the mistake. She shook off the minor irritation and refocused on her task, trying to recapture her excitement.

This would be her second voyage as a shipowner. Her first, completed two weeks ago, had been a direct back-and-forth trade deal that had let her and the crew grow accustomed to one another. It had gone . . . fine. Oh, the profits had been good, and the crew appreciated that. The deals she negotiated were their livelihood.

Yet there was something about the sailors, and their captain, that Rysn hadn't yet figured out. Some hesitance to engage with her. Perhaps they were simply accustomed to Vstim and not Rysn, as her ways were slightly different from her babsk's. Or maybe they wanted a voyage more engaging, more rewarding, than such a simple trip.

She sifted through her options, eventually settling on three different trade offers. Any of the three could be lucrative, but which to select? She mulled it over for a time, then wrote out a list of pros and cons to each deal, as Vstim had taught her.

Eventually she rubbed her temples, her eyebrow jewelry tinkling softly, and decided to give it a few minutes. Instead she reached for some spanreed communications that had come in recently—from women around the world who, like her, had lost the use of their legs.

Talking with them was exciting and invigorating. They felt so many of her own emotions, and were eager to share with her things they'd learned. Mura, an Azish woman, had designed several interesting devices to help in daily life, demonstrating marvelous creativity. Hooks and rings—with items hanging on pegs—to allow for ready access. Specialized hoops, wires, and curved rods to aid in dressing herself.

Reading through the latest letters, she couldn't help but be encouraged. She had once felt so isolated. Now she realized there were many people who—despite being strangely invisible to the world at large—faced her same challenges. Their stories invigorated her, and with their suggestions in hand, Rysn had ordered changes to her ship. A fixed seat and sunshade up on the quarterdeck, near the helm station. Changes to her cabin to make moving around and dressing easier.

During the ship's time in port, the carpenters were doing as she'd asked. Yet there had been so many confused looks. And that same awful question.

"But why?"

Why not stay behind and let an underling do

the in-person negotiations? She could negotiate via spanreed for the true contract. Why did she want a station up on the quarterdeck, rather than making the voyage comfortable in her cabin? Why ask about a pulley system to get herself up and down from the quarterdeck, when there were porters who could carry her?

Why, why, why? Why do you want to live, Rysn? Why do you want to better your situation? She scanned the drawings that Mura had sent her. It was a recent design, done by an ardent in Jah Keved, for a different kind of wheeled chair. Rysn used the common type, with small wheels on the rear legs. It needed a porter who could tip the chair back—like she was in a reverse wheelbarrow—and push her where she needed to go. The design had been used for centuries.

But here was something new. A chair with large wheels you could move *yourself* with your hands. She'd need to have one of these commissioned. It wouldn't be of much use on a ship—and the streets of Thaylen City were probably too rough, with too many steps—but if only she could get from room to room in her own house, so many things would change.

She wrote a reply to Mura, then revisited her three possible trips, weighing them. A shipment of fish oil, some rugs, or some water barrels. All three were just so *mundane*. Her ship, the *Wandersail*, had been built for grander things. Granted, with the war, even simple trips were now dangerous. But she'd been trained by the best in the business to search for the opportunities no one else would take.

Search for the need, Vstim had always taught her. *Don't be a barnacle, simply leeching money where you can, Rysn. Find the unmet desire. . . .*

She decided to start over, but was interrupted by a quiet knock at her outer door. She looked up with surprise; she'd not been expecting company. Nikli, after glancing for her approval, moved out into the antechamber to answer the knock.

A smiling man entered her office a second later. Rysn dropped her papers in shock.

The Reshi man had deep tan skin, with his hair in two long braids down over his shoulders. Talik wore a traditional Reshi wrap and tasseled overshirt, with his chest bare. She knew, from their two years of communication, that he generally wore one of several fine Thaylen suits when traveling. When he put on his traditional clothing, it was to deliberately remind people where he was from.

Seeing him left her speechless. He lived thousands of miles away from her. How was he here? She stammered, searching for what to say.

"Ah, so now that you're a powerful shipowner," he said, "you have no further words for one such as me? I guess I'll be off then. . . ." He said it with a widening grin, however.

"Get in here and sit down," she said, scooting down the table toward the far end, where it wasn't so cluttered with papers. She waved for him to sit in a chair across the long table from her. "How on Roshar did you get here so quickly? I wrote to you only three days ago!"

"We were already in Azimir," he explained, settling down. "The king wants to meet this Dalinar Kholin and see these Knights Radiant for himself."

"The king *left* Relu-na?" Rysn asked. She felt her jaw drop.

"Strange times," Talik said. "With nightmares walking the world, and the Vorin peoples uniting under one banner—an Alethi one no less—it was time."

"They . . . We aren't under an Alethi banner," she said. "We are a united coalition. Here, let me pour you some tea."

She took her grabbing stick and used it to hook the teapot by the handle to drag it across the table toward them. Talik—who had been so stern when they'd first met so long ago—leaped to his feet to help. He took the teapot and poured two cups.

She was grateful. And also frustrated. Not being

able to walk was annoying, and *that* emotion people seemed to understand. But few understood the sense of embarrassment she felt—despite knowing she shouldn't—at being a burden. While she appreciated the concern people showed for her, she worked so hard to be able to do things on her own. When people accidentally undercut that, it became more difficult to ignore the part of her that whispered lies. That told her that because she was less capable in a few areas, she was worthless in general.

She was doing better about that lately. She didn't have shamespren hanging around these days. But she still wanted to find the right way to explain she wasn't some child who needed to be coddled.

"Gods far and near," Talik said as he handed her a cup, then sat back down. "I can't believe how the time passes. It's been . . . what, two *years* since you first visited us? Since your accident? Feels like only a few months ago."

"Feels like an eternity for me," Rysn said, sipping her tea and stretching her other hand out on the desk toward Chiri-Chiri. Normally, the larkin would hop over and sniff it when she did that. Today she barely stirred, letting out a soft chirp.

"I suppose we can catch up later," Talik said. "For now, can I see her?"

Rysn nodded, setting aside the tea and scooting

over to scoop up the larkin. Chiri-Chiri batted her wings a few times, then settled down. Rysn held her so Talik could see, after pulling his chair around the table to settle down next to her.

"I've shown her to many animal doctors," Rysn said, "and they are baffled. Everyone thought the larkin were extinct, if they'd even heard of one before."

Talik reached to carefully touch Chiri-Chiri along the top of her head. "So big . . ." he whispered. "I had not realized."

"What do you mean?" Rysn asked.

"When Aimia fell," he explained, "the Na-Alind—a family among the greatshelled gods of the Reshi—took in the last of the larkin. Greatshells do not think or speak like people do, and the ways of our gods are strange. But best we can tell, there was a promise among them. To protect these, their cousins.

"I have seen only two other larkin. They were both decades old, but were small, no longer than a person's hand."

"Chiri-Chiri likes to eat," Rysn said. "A lot. At least she used to. . . ."

"In ancient times, larkin grew to larger sizes," Talik said. "They're supposed to remain small these days. Hidden. Lest men hunt them again."

"But what do I *do*?" Rysn asked. "How do I help her?"

"When we received your letter three days ago," Talik said, "I wrote to those on the island. The king's consort approached Relu-na. The answer is simple, Rysn, but not easy. Not easy at all."

"What?"

Talik met her eyes. "The island said to take her home."

"To the Reshi Isles? I suppose I can go for a visit. How did you get through the occupied territory? The long way around to the east? We . . ." She trailed off, seeing his grim expression. "Oh. By her 'home,' you mean Aimia. Well, that's not impossible. The Royal Navy has set up a few outposts on the main island."

"Not the main island of Aimia, Rysn," Talik said. "You need to take her to Akinah. The lost city." He shook his head. "It is an impossible voyage. No one has stepped foot on the island in generations."

Rysn frowned, stroking Chiri-Chiri and thinking. Akinah. Hadn't she read that name recently? She gestured to Talik, then set Chiri-Chiri down and scooted back to her papers.

She found what she was looking for a few minutes later. "Here," she said, holding it so he could lean down beside her and read. He didn't ascribe to Vorin prohibitions on that. And, well, neither did Rysn, for all the fact that she wore a glove these days without complaint.

A ghost ship was discovered by a Thaylen military vessel some two months ago. Officials had traced it back to a voyage to the semi-mythical city of Akinah. The Queen of Urithiru, Navani Kholin, had put out a request for another ship to travel to Aimia and investigate a certain region. A strange storm where the ruins of Akinah were rumored to be found.

Queen Navani promised a reward to those who were willing, but so far none had taken up the offer. Rysn looked to Talik, who nodded encouragingly.

It seemed that Rysn needed to pay a visit to Urithiru.

2

Rysn was met at Urithiru by a master-servant guide and four porters: an envoy from Brightness Navani, meant to show that Rysn was expected and her visit appreciated. The porters carried a single-person palanquin, which they set down. They inspected her wheeled chair.

"Brightness Rysn," Nikli said from behind the chair, "prefers to use her own chair as transportation."

While that was true, Nikli had—despite trying hard—gotten it wrong again. "I am honored by this envoy," Rysn said. "Nikli, they know Urithiru far better than we do. Best if we let them carry me. I would appreciate it, however, if you brought the chair along in case it's needed later."

"Of course, Brightness," he said, sounding embarrassed. She hated making the correction, but these men would consider it a personal duty to serve her. Rysn had learned that accepting hospitality was important for trade negotiations.

She had Nikli transfer her to the palanquin. Once in, she shoved down the feelings of insecurity and worthlessness that still cropped up whenever she was handled like a sack of lavis grain.

No feeling sorry for yourself, she thought forcefully. *You filled your quota on that months ago.*

Once she was settled, Nikli opened Chiri-Chiri's basket so Rysn could scoop up the larkin and put her inside. Despite his occasional misstep, Nikli was doing a commendable job of anticipating her needs. He'd figure out the details as they spent more time together.

"Thank you, Nikli," she said.

"We'll be right behind, Brightness, if you need anything."

The Alethi porters marched her down the Oathgate's ramp, palanquin drapes open so she could survey the landscape. Urithiru—the mighty tower city of the Knights Radiant—had ten platforms out in front of it, each connected via Oathgate to a different city across the world. But the true marvel was the tower itself: built into the mountains, ten tiers reaching high toward the sun. They said it was nearly two *hundred* stories tall. How did the lower levels not collapse under the weight?

Curiously, not all of this city's wonders were ancient. Rysn kept keen watch for the secret Alethi project Vstim had told her about. As she was carried onto the plateau that connected the ten Oathgate ramps, she spotted it. The plateau had sheer cliffs at both sides, where engineers were constructing two large wooden platforms.

Officially, it was said to be an enormous lift. Connected by conjoined fabrials in new ways devised by Navani Kholin, when one side lowered, the other rose. Rysn—privileged in her relationship to her babsk, who was Thaylen Minister of Trade—had heard *extremely* interesting talk of the hidden purpose behind these platforms.

If what she'd heard was true . . . If those fabrials could do what Queen Navani claimed they could . . .

Chiri-Chiri shifted in her arms, then peeked her sleek crustacean head out the window. She made an inquisitive clicking sound.

"You find it interesting?" Rysn said, hopeful.

Chiri-Chiri chirped.

"There are a lot of fabrials in this tower," Rysn noted. "If you start eating them like you did last time, I'll have to lock you away again. Fair warning."

Rysn wasn't certain how much Chiri-Chiri understood. The little creature did seem to be able to sense Rysn's tone, and sometimes responded accordingly—depending on how mischievous she was feeling. Today she only nestled back down and returned to sleep. So lethargic. Rysn's heart nearly broke.

To distract herself, Rysn set Chiri-Chiri on a pillow, then took notes on what she saw in Urithiru. Much was the same as her last visit: a wide variety of ethnicities mingling in the crowded hallways. Her master-servant guide answered questions and explained the architecture as they walked, eventually reaching the tower atrium with its enormous glass window displaying a frozen wasteland. Rysn couldn't help wondering at the implications of this place. It wasn't every day that a new kingdom was founded, let alone one in the mythical city of the Knights Radiant.

The palanquin was small enough to navigate through hallways, so it fit with her porters on one of the marvelous fabrial lifts in the atrium. Up she went, tens of stories. At the top, Rysn's porters carried her into a small chamber where Navani Kholin—recently crowned queen of Urithiru—was taking meetings. She was an intimidating woman with her Alethi height, her black and grey hair done in intricate braids atop her head and woven with glowing sapphires.

Most of Rysn's contemporaries entered a discussion asking, "What can I get from this?" Rysn had been disabused of that notion early in her training. *Her* babsk taught a different way of seeing the world, training her to ask, "What need can I fulfill?"

That was the true purpose of a merchant. To find complementary needs, then bridge the distance between them so everyone benefited. It wasn't about what you could get *from* people, but what you could get *for* them that made a successful merchant.

And everyone had needs. Even queens.

The porters set Rysn down, and she left Chiri-Chiri in the palanquin, having Nikli transfer her to the chair before Navani's desk. She preferred to use the seats offered her in these situations, though her wheeled chair was carefully stowed at the back of the room.

The porters and guide retreated, though Nikli remained right inside the door to wait upon her needs. A young woman stood at a writing desk nearby, recording minutes, and two guards watched the door. Aside from that, Rysn was virtually alone beneath the gaze of this incredibly regal woman.

It was a good thing Rysn had mostly gotten over her feelings of insecurity. Otherwise this might have been very intimidating, instead of only slightly so. Navani studied Rysn as if she were a schematic for a ship, seeming to read her very soul with those discerning eyes.

"So . . ." the queen said in Thaylen. "Who are you again?"

"Brightness?" Rysn said. "Er, I'm Rysn Ftori. Bah-Vstim? I came in response to your request?"

"Oh, right," Navani said. "The ghost ship." Navani held out her palm, and her assistant hurried over, handing her the appropriate notes. The queen stood and paced as she read through the notes while Rysn waited.

Finally the queen stopped, focused on the chair at the rear of the room, then pulled her chair over and sat before Rysn. It was a small gesture, but appreciated. Rysn didn't mind when people remained standing in her presence, but there was a certain thoughtfulness in the way Navani situated herself so they could discuss at eye level with one another.

"Queen Fen says you have inspected the ship in person?" Navani said.

"Yes, Brightness," Rysn said. "I visited it yesterday, after I decided to agree to your request. It was brought into port weeks ago, and has been undergoing repairs. I toured it to see if I could notice anything odd."

Navani's eyes flicked toward the wheeled chair.

"I was carried, Brightness," Rysn said. "With my porters, I assure you I am quite mobile."

"You know," Navani said, "we have Radiants who specialize in something called Regrowth...."

"My injury turned out to be too old for healing, Brightness," Rysn said, her stomach twisting at the words. "I tried to avail myself of their abilities the moment I learned of them."

"Of course," Navani said. "I'm sorry."

"No need to apologize for offering me aid, Brightness," Rysn said. *In fact, I'm glad you noticed. Because there's something else you might do for me.* But the time for negotiation had not yet arrived.

Rysn had a need. Several of them. Best to find out what Navani needed, and why, before they began the dance. "If we may return to the topic at hand, Your Majesty . . ."

"Yes," Navani said. "This ship. So curious. Did you find anything interesting in your inspection?"

"Whoever set the ship adrift tried to scuttle it," Rysn said. "But they weren't aware that modern Thaylen ships aren't so easily sunk by a hole or two in the hull. It's obvious foul play, Brightness. The logbooks were taken."

"Blood on the deck?" Navani asked.

"None we could find, Brightness."

"And . . . the missing Soulcaster?" Navani asked.

Rysn had only just been told this particular piece of intelligence: the ghost ship, *First Dreams*, had carried a rogue Soulcaster as a passenger. Not a Knight Radiant, but a woman trained in the use of one of the ancient devices that could transform things from one material to another.

"We didn't find the Soulcaster," Rysn said. "Neither the woman nor the device. It seems likely that someone knew the ship was carrying this runaway, and then attacked it, murdering the crew to get the Soulcaster."

The devices were rare and extremely powerful. Most kingdoms had access to only a handful of Soulcasters—if any at all. Many people in Thaylenah thought the Alethi's wartime prowess was due less to superior troops, and more to the number of Soulcasters they had feeding said troops.

It wasn't the kind of thing one pointed out to one's allies. Particularly not while in a joint large-scale war against ancient monsters from the Void.

"Yes . . . perhaps," Navani said, rolling her notes and tapping them softly against her other hand. "I have spoken to the prince of Liafor, who says the Soulcaster thought that Aimia—as the ancient home of Soulcasters—might contain secrets to healing her afflictions. More, the ship's captain—a man named

Vazrmeb—was infatuated with the legendary riches of Akinah, the lost capital of Aimia."

Curious. That was more than Vstim knew. The queen appeared as resourceful as her reputation implied.

"Aimia is barren," Rysn said carefully. "It's been thoroughly scouted, and hundreds of captains— with stars in their eyes—have tried finding mysterious fortunes on the island. They've all returned empty-handed."

"From the large island, yes," Navani said. "But what of the smaller ones surrounding it? What of the hidden one, shrouded in mystery and storm?"

"The Rock of Secrets," Rysn said. "The mythical Akinah. Some say it is only a legend."

"They said the same about Urithiru," Navani said. "Some scholars think the ruins they've found in other locations are remnants of the city, but their evidence is weak. Our Windrunners report a strange weather pattern surrounding a specific place in the ocean there, the very place the ghost ship was said to have been on course to visit before falling.

"I'm convinced Akinah *is* hidden inside that strange weather pattern. Either way, we need to investigate. My husband worries the winds might veil an enemy fortress."

"Your Windrunners reported?" Rysn said. "So . . .

why not have them fly down and investigate?" This was the item from the request that most confused her, the one that had made her come to Urithiru to ask in person. Why did the Knights Radiant need the help of a common sailing vessel?

"There is . . . something on that island," Navani said. "Something that is able to undermine the powers of the Knights Radiant. My soldiers reported seeing swarms of small shadows darting through the clouds. And legends about Aimia speak of mythical creatures that feed off Stormlight."

Reflexively, Rysn glanced toward the palanquin and Chiri-Chiri inside. Navani watched her, calm, her lips cocked slightly to the side. She knew. Well, of course she did. Rysn hadn't tried to keep Chiri-Chiri hidden—and the little larkin wouldn't have let her if she had.

"May I see the creature?" Navani asked. "I promise I won't try to separate it from you."

Well, Rysn had known this conversation would be difficult for her to steer. You couldn't always negotiate from a position of power. So she waved for Nikli to pick Chiri-Chiri up and carry her over.

As the months had passed, Rysn had begun to truly grasp the strategic importance of Stormlight as a fuel both for fabrials and for the Knights Radiant. Beyond that, the enemy had creatures—known as Fused—who used the Void's own Light. Chiri-Chiri fed on that just as eagerly as Stormlight.

Was the strange creature she kept as a pet something more dangerous, and more important, than she'd ever stopped to consider? Rysn took Chiri-Chiri, who stood up, then lifted her wings. A sleek monster in miniature—despite her wan carapace, she was as majestic as any greatshell. Indeed, Chiri-Chiri seemed more energetic than she had earlier. Perhaps she was feeling better.

A few awespren, like rings of blue smoke, appeared around Navani as she leaned down. "It's gorgeous," she whispered. "And does it really . . ."

As if in response, Chiri-Chiri clicked and took to the air, her wings beating quickly. She flew across the room to the wall where she grasped hold of the lamp fixture. Rysn put her hand to her face as—without so much as a click of embarrassment—Chiri-Chiri ingested the Stormlight in the lamp, darkening the room significantly.

"I'm sorry, Brightness," Rysn said. "We've been trying to work on *not* eating lights inside fixtures. She's been feeling sick lately though, and has been regressing."

Navani merely watched with wide eyes. She brought out a few diamond chips and scattered them on her table. Fortunately, Chiri-Chiri saw these as easier prey, and dropped to the table with a thump to begin ingesting their Light. After consuming a few, she mouthed one of the spheres and began to play with it, rolling it away, then hopping over and catching it in her mouth before it could fall off the desk.

"Is this it?" Navani whispered. "The way the Thaylen artifabrians can so carefully adjust the Stormlight in their fabrials? Do your people have dozens of these beasts hidden away?"

"What?" Rysn said. "No, Brightness. I was given Chiri-Chiri on a trading expedition in the Reshi Isles. She's the only one I've ever seen; an oddity, not a secret weapon."

"Still, I should very much like a chance to study one of these," Navani said.

By reflex, Rysn began to reach toward Chiri-Chiri—to scoop her up. Rysn restrained herself, but the queen noticed. She didn't repeat her promise not to take Chiri-Chiri, and she didn't need to. Rysn trusted her, well enough. Navani Kholin wasn't a thief. But she *was* a woman who usually got what she wanted, eventually.

Hopefully there was another way to fill *that* need.

"My notes say you possess an extraordinary ship," Navani said. "The storm around Akinah is terrible and persistent. Do you think your ship could penetrate it?"

"If any ship can," Rysn said, "it will be the *Wandersail*. We have fabrial pumps and modern storm stabilizers. But your information worries me. A place Radiants are afraid to visit? I must care for the well-being of my crew."

"I understand," Navani said, "but I can't risk sending Windrunners alone if they will be drained midflight and fall into the ocean to drown. And so, I need a ship. I think you'll find that your own queen encourages this mission as well.

"Hopefully we can minimize the danger. All I want is for you to take one of my scribes to the place, penetrate the storm, and let her survey the location. It shouldn't take her more than a day to complete her inspection and collect a few artifacts. After that, you can return. I'll see you properly outfitted beforehand and compensated afterward."

Navani handed her a paper with generous payment terms. Rysn didn't miss the promise of traditional salvage payments to the crew, if anything valuable was located. Even without that, she was thrilled at the numbers. If she'd been forced to visit Akinah on her own, she'd have needed to arrange for many nearby merchant stops—trading goods along the way to earn maintenance for the ship and crew. But with a patron, they could take a direct course.

She longed to do something adventurous like

this. During her years training with her babsk, she'd complained incessantly about the way he'd dragged her all across Roshar. She had expected her apprenticeship to bring her to rich customers, trading for silks in courts and palaces. Instead she'd visited one backwater after another, going all the difficult places no one else thought worth the effort.

It was a constant source of amazement that her babsk hadn't tossed her overboard after a single day— let alone hundreds—listening to her complain. Now that she was older, she found herself sincerely *missing* those excursions. To go somewhere new? To investigate the trading opportunities on a mythical island? And to possibly save Chiri-Chiri in the process? The prospect thrilled her.

There were still problems, however.

"Brightness," Rysn said, "I have a good crew, seasoned and well-traveled. But you need to understand, sailors can be superstitious. The fact that we'd be sailing to a forbidden island so soon after the discovery of a ghost ship returning from that location . . . well, I have spent an entire day pondering how to sell them on the idea. It's daunting."

"I could send you a Radiant or two to improve morale," Navani said.

"That *would* help," Rysn said. "Could you also ask

something of Queen Fen? You said she would want this mission to take place. A personal request from our own queen to my sailors would mean a lot to them. It would transform this voyage from a simple job into a royal mandate."

Plus, it would help with Rysn's authority on the ship. She shouldn't need that, but after the curious way she'd been treated on her first voyage . . . well, she would appreciate the queen's mandate to help prop her up.

"It will be done," Navani said. "Queen Fen and I have been talking for some time about an expedition like this, so I'm certain she would be willing to write to your sailors." Navani's eyes narrowed. "But what of you, Captain? This *is* a difficult mission I propose. Is my payment offer enough? Is there anything more I could offer the woman who owns her own ship and keeps a mythical creature as a pet?"

Rysn glanced at Chiri-Chiri, who had grown tired of playing already, and was quietly batting at the sphere instead of chewing on it. She noticed Rysn, then launched into the air—flying to the palanquin to rest.

Needs. And connections.

"I should be honest, Brightness," Rysn said. "Chiri-Chiri . . . is not well. I believe this mission could help her, so I am eager to undertake it for that reason. I need no special payment. However, if you're willing to listen, there *is* something I would ask of you."

"Speak freely," Navani said.

The way Chiri-Chiri flew . . . What would it be like to be so free? Unchained? "Is it true," Rysn asked, "that you have developed platforms that can soar high in the air?"

"Yes," Navani said. "We use them for archer stations on battlefields."

"But you're trying to do more than that, aren't you? Like with the construction outside, the supposed lifts?"

"I have shared my plans with Queen Fen," Navani said. "I'm not certain what more you want me to . . ." She trailed off, perhaps noticing that Rysn had turned from Chiri-Chiri to instead stare at something else: her wheeled chair.

It provided her with some measure of liberty, but still required someone to push it for her. She looked forward to getting the one with large wheels she could move on her own. But that design, despite being wonderful, was so bulky. Plus, few current roads and floors were built for someone to be wheeled across. Even moving under her own power, her ability to get around would be severely limited.

Was there instead a way to soar? Perhaps never as well as Chiri-Chiri, but almost anything would be an upgrade from the chair. Her source of freedom, but also a constant reminder that the world did not accommodate people like her.

"I have scholars working on some prototypes that might interest you," Navani said. "Since I'm sending a scribe on this mission anyway, I could arrange for her to be one who is experienced with our new fabrial designs. She could run some experiments for me on the ship, and perhaps show you what is possible with this technology."

"I would find that agreeable, Brightness," Rysn said. "And these other terms are generous and accepted. Consider our deal sealed. The *Wandersail* is at your disposal."

3

The Lopen had never known there were so many
different types of people in the world.

Oh, he'd expected there to be a lot, sure. But not
so *many*. At Urithiru, you could see them all. How
they dressed, how they talked, how they ate. Today,
he zoomed past men from Steen with their beards
wrapped in cords to make them long like a sausage.
Women from Tashikk, wearing colorful wraps. Traders from New Natanan, with blue to their skin, as if
they had sapphires in their veins.

All so different. He figured, sure, that people must
be like mountains. See, when you were far away from
mountains, they all basically looked the same. Fly
up high, soar over them in a hurry, and there was no
time for detail. Pointed. Covered in snow. Mountain.
Got it.

Fly up close, and they each had their own distinctive jagged bits and places where the rock showed through. He'd even found *flowers* growing on a few, near vents that let out warm air. The problem with people was that everyone saw other nations from far away. Saw them as big mountainous blobs. Foreigners. Strange. Got it.

Up close, it was hard to see people that way. Each was so distinctive. Everyone should use a "the" in front of their name. He'd merely figured that out first.

Rua, his spren, darted out of a side corridor ahead, then spun around in a loop, excited. Looked like he'd found the Reshi people Lopen was supposed to meet with today. Great! Lopen increased his speed with a Lashing, soaring a couple feet over the heads of the people in the corridor. Some of them cringed with startled expressions. He was doing them a favor, sure, because they *should* be used to Windrunners flying overhead. What did they expect him to do? *Walk?*

Rua transformed into one of his favorite shapes—a flying chull with broad wings—and zoomed alongside Lopen. At the next intersection, Rua led him left. They emerged into the atrium: a big open section that seemed to have no roof, just tens upon tens of levels with balconies and a large window.

Here, Lopen finally found his Reshi visitors.

Storms! How'd they gotten so far inside in such a short time? "Nice work, naco," he said to Rua, then Lashed himself downward so he landed near the visitors.

He strode toward them, hands out. "Greetings! And I am the Lopen, Windrunner, poet, and your most humble servant. You must be King Ral-na!"

He'd been warned the king would be the one in the robes. He was a short man with greying hair, though his robes parted down the front to show firm pectoral muscles. He was attended by a group of fierce men in wraps, carrying spears.

"I speak for the king," one of them said in pretty good Alethi. The tall figure wore his hair in two long braids. "You may call me Talik."

"Sure, Talik!" Lopen said. "Do you like to fly?"

"I wouldn't be able to say," Talik replied. "Were you the one who was supposed to—"

"We can talk," Lopen said, "*later.*" He grabbed Talik by the arm, infused him, waved to the others, then launched the two of them high into the air.

They shot up along the window, passing story after story. Lopen hung on tight. This Talik fellow was an important official, and it wouldn't do to drop him or something. He was surrounded by shock-spren in the shape of pale yellow triangles. So he seemed to be enjoying the ride.

"Now see, I figure that you live on a giant crab out in the ocean, right?" Lopen said as they flew. "One of the *really* big ones. A bigger-than-a-town type crab.

"I had a cousin once, sure, who had a crab he swore had bred with chulls, but I didn't think that was possible, even if it came up to my knees. So it was a big storming crab. But we couldn't build a *house* on its back. That's *wild*, velo. You deserve *respect* for living on a giant crab. Who lives on a crab? No regular people. Just people like *you*."

Lopen slowed them near the top, where the atrium finally ended, maybe a thousand feet in the air or more. It provided the best view out the window: an amazing field of snow-tipped mountains. Lopen could appreciate, from up here, how they all looked the same. One shouldn't forget that they weren't, sure, but there *was* a perspective from a distance—different from the up-close perspective.

Up close, differences could chafe. But if you remembered that from far away you all looked the same . . . well, that was important too.

"What is this?" Talik demanded. "Are you trying to intimidate me?"

"Intimidate?" Lopen said, then glanced to Rua, who grew six arms and used all of them to smack his forehead at the stupidity of that idea. "Velo," Lopen said to Talik, "you live up high on a giant crab. I figured you'd *like* heights."

"They don't frighten me," Talik said, folding his arms.

"Yeah, good. See, look. The view is great, right? Something you've never seen, right? I know about the Reshi Sea—my cousin, he lived out on the coast, and I've heard him say how hot it is there. No snow."

Talik regarded him as they both hung in the air. Then the man turned and peered out the window, inspecting the beautiful field of mountains. "That . . . is rather spectacular."

"*See?*" Lopen said. "I told Kaladin, 'I'm gonna fly those Reshi guys up high.' And Kaladin said, 'I don't think that's a good—' but I didn't let him finish, because he was going to grumble, so I said, 'No, I got this, gancho. They're gonna *love* it.' And you love it."

"I . . . don't know what to make of you," Talik admitted.

"Nah, velo, you do. I'm the Lopen." He pointed at himself. Rua appeared to Talik and gestured with the six arms, then grew two more for effect. "So what do you think? Should I fly your king up here? I was a king for, sure, only a couple of hours. So I don't *really* know what kings like."

"You . . . were a king?"

"For two hours," Lopen said. "It's a long story. But my arm was newly regrown then, so for a while that arm had only been a king. Never not a king. Wild, eh?"

Talik looked down, then waggled his feet. "How long . . ."

"Oh, you're safe," Lopen said. "If you drop, it would take *way* long for you to hit. I'd catch you first."

"That's not terribly encouraging . . ." Talik said. He took a deep breath, then studied Lopen. "Normally, I would assume a person who brought me up here like this had done so to discomfort me during our negotiations. But you . . . really aren't doing that, are you?"

"We can go down if you want," Lopen said. "I just thought . . . I mean, you like it, right?"

"I do," Talik said, then smiled. "I will admit to finding myself . . . encouraged by the presence of a Herdazian among the Knights Radiant. I lived among your people for several years, Windrunner. Let me ask you this. In your opinion, do they truly care about us? The Alethi, the Vedens, the Azish? For centuries, they've ignored us in the Isles. Now, amid a war, they write to us? They ask for a meeting with our king?

"We are a proud people, the Lopen—but small, insignificant. Paid attention to by outsiders for our novelty, or for the ways we can be exploited. I trained in Thaylenah. I know how we're regarded. And I know they have historically treated you the same way. So can you tell me why the greatest kings in Roshar would suddenly show interest in us?"

"Oh, that," Lopen said. "Yeah, they think maybe the enemy will start moving troops through the sea to land for an invasion of Jah Keved in the east. So, Dalinar and Jasnah figure it would be good to have you on their side."

"So it's purely political," Talik said.

"Purely?" Lopen shrugged, and Rua did too. "They're trying to be good, velo. But they're, you know, Alethi. Conquering folks is basically their primary cultural heritage. It's taking some time for them to learn to see things another way—but they are listening. They agreed to let me talk to you, after I explained we were practically cousins, what with the Reshi Isles being so close to Herdaz."

Talik nodded.

"I was one of the ones that told them to send to you," Lopen said. "See, lots of us people—Herdaz, Reshi, even Thaylenah to an extent—are small. But the whole world has been invaded, not only the big places. And a lot of small people make big numbers, velo. That's why I wanted to talk to you first, to ask you to listen to what the Alethi say."

"I will suggest to the king that he accept your advice, the Lopen," Talik said, then extended his hand. "I appreciate your sincerity. It is not what I expected to find in this city."

Lopen took the hand.

"Before you take me down," Talik said, "I have a . . . somewhat delicate question for you. Our king, who is one of my parents, has undergone some unusual physical changes lately. They have transformed him in dramatic ways, and at first we thought it was a gift of our god, as he was not born looking as he does now. We now realize this transformation is in relation to a spren he has been seeing. It is why he agreed to make this long trip."

"Your king is Radiant!" Lopen said. "What kind?"

"He can make the very air seem to catch flame," Talik said. "And sees a spren that burns through the inside of objects in curious treelike patterns."

"Dustbringer," Lopen said. "We've been *hoping* to find some more. Look, this is great. But don't talk to the ones we already have, all right? It's complicated, but we'd love to see you figure your own way, without anyone interfering."

"I do not understand."

"I don't really either," Lopen said. "Have your king talk to Dalinar about it, all right? But *don't* tell anyone else. It's politics. The annoying kind."

"There's another kind?"

Lopen grinned. "I like you, velo." He grabbed Talik by the arm and flew him to the floor—where a number of his friends were arguing loudly with some of Dalinar's soldiers. They were all surrounded by pools of angerspren and gesturing at the sky. Poor guys. Probably sad they didn't get to fly too.

Kaladin had arrived, so Lopen towed Talik over and presented him. "This is my cousin Talik," Lopen said, pointing. "He's, sure, the king's son. Treat him well, gancho."

"I'll try," Kaladin said, his voice dry. "I hope Lopen's tour of the tower was informative."

"Tour . . . ?" Talik said, glancing at Lopen, who made some low-key shushing gestures. Wasn't Lopen's fault he'd spent too long at lunch and hadn't managed to greet the Reshi when they arrived. He blamed Cord's cooking. "Yes . . ." Talik continued. "It was informative."

"Excellent," Kaladin said. "I have scheduled a meeting for your king with Dalinar and Navani Kholin, rulers of this tower. Though perhaps we should first deal with whatever is happening over there. . . ." He pointed at the Reshi king's arguing soldiers. Talik rushed over to calm them, though Kaladin lingered with Lopen.

"Where is Huio?" Kaladin asked.

"He was busy. So I went on my own."

Kaladin gave him a long-suffering look. Huio and Lopen had persuaded him that the Reshi would respond best to Herdazians meeting them, and that was true. So why was he having a problem?

"I had counted," Kaladin said, "on Huio reining you in a little, Lopen. You didn't do anything stupid, did you? You did *ask* before you flew him up high, right?"

"Um . . ."

"Lopen," Kaladin said softly. "You *need* to start thinking more about what you do and say. Please. Be more careful."

"I will," Lopen promised quickly. "Look, everything turned out all right, gancho! That Talik fellow, he's a good one. Take care of him. These Reshi have a secret you'll find interesting, and they might tell you, if you're nice."

"What? Why don't you tell me?"

"Can't, gancho," Lopen said. "They told me in confidence."

"Lopen," Kaladin said with another of his long-suffering captain-of-the-world sighs. "You were sent *specifically* to do reconnaissance on this group."

"Sure, and I did. But I can't betray their secrets. They're my cousins, gon."

"They're *not* your cousins."

"Herdaz is next to Reshi. So we're cousins."

"Alethkar is next to Herdaz too," Kaladin said. "So *I'm* as much your cousin as those people are."

Lopen tapped him on the shoulder and winked. "You're finally figuring it out, gancho. Good job."

"Well, I suppose that's beside the point. I want to ask you something. The queen needs me to send some Windrunners on a mission to—"

"Oh!" Lopen said. "Pick me. I wanna do it."

"You don't even know what the mission is, Lopen."

"Still volunteering," Lopen said. "Sounds special."

"We're sending another mission to Akinah."

"The place where Leyten got dropped into the ocean?" Lyn and Sigzil had barely managed to rescue him after something sucked away his Stormlight.

"Same," Kaladin said. "We don't have a lot of resources to spare at the moment, but Navani is convinced something important is hiding on that island. So we're sending a scouting mission via ship. I suggested we send Windrunners who could swim, just in case. That means you and Huio."

"Pick me!"

"I literally just did."

"I know. That was for old time's sake."

"Navani's sending a scribe," Kaladin continued,

"and you should listen to her advice. Also, I was thinking it might be good to send Rock. He's one of the only other members of Bridge Four who can swim, and Leyten's report included seeing strange spren in the clouds. They might be involved with whatever is leeching Stormlight. It would be nice to have him along to see Voidspren, if they try to remain hidden."

"Rock won't go," Lopen said. "Next week's his anniversary with his wife. We can take Cord. She can see spren too, and she wants to see more of the world. Besides, Rua likes her."

Kaladin glanced toward the honorspren, who was bouncing along the ground in the shape of a full-sized axehound. "Lopen. I'm worried about this mission. Something about it doesn't feel right. I'd go myself, but . . ."

Lopen understood. Kaladin already had to divide his time between the battlefronts in southern Alethkar and Azir. Plus he had to organize patrols to watch the coalition fleets from above, *and* see to training here in the tower. The numbers of Windrunners were swelling, now that so many of the original crew were picking up their own squires.

It was a lot for one man to track. They were long past the point where Kaladin could go with every team to watch them personally. It seemed to be tearing him apart inside to let go.

"Hey, gancho," Lopen said, his hand on Kaladin's shoulder. "I'll make sure everyone comes back, all right? Don't you worry."

"Make sure *you* come back too," Kaladin said. "Go talk to Huio and Cord and see if they're willing. Then report to Rushu, the ardent you'll be accompanying. She has information on some secret details of your mission that I don't want to discuss in public. After that, have your team travel to Thaylen City via Oathgate and report to the docks tomorrow morning. And be careful."

"Gancho, I'm *always* careful."

"Are you?"

"Of course," he said, pointing at himself. "What? You think *this* happens by accident?" He grinned, waved Rua over, then went to taunt Huio about being sent on a special mission—before relenting and telling him that he got to go too.

4

Rysn had been warned never to mistake Thaylen naval *traditions* for Thaylen naval *regulations*. Regulations, after all, were written down—which made them far, *far* easier to change. She considered this as Nikli and his assistant brought her aboard the *Wandersail*. Her ship. And not her ship. Both at the same time.

It was an *incredible* craft. Full-rigged, built for speed from light—but strong—Soulcast wood. It had ballistae with attached firepods for setting aflame enemy ships, and could drop sails quickly and maneuver with oars if faced by the same. It was fearsome in war, swift in trade. And a part of Rysn still couldn't believe she owned it.

And she did. Rysn was its master, though owner-ship of Thaylen merchant ships could be complex.

Vstim, her teacher and friend, had ordered the ship built, but had accepted investment funds from several others. Since he was now Minister of Trade, he'd given the ship to her—transferring ownership while remaining the primary investor.

A large part of its profits would go to the investors, including Vstim or his heirs—but he had given *her* the writ of ownership, and the symbolic captain's cord to hang with her colors. That was the strictest definition of ownership, and no one would dispute it.

And yet, she had never touched the ship's wheel. She wasn't so innocent as to assume that she'd be able to helm the ship herself, but Vstim—when they'd been on voyages together—had usually been offered the chance to steer the ship for a short time near the start of the voyage. A symbolic ritual, but one he had always seemed to enjoy.

Rysn had asked for the same privilege on her first voyage last month. She hadn't realized that her babsk had *earned* this privilege over years of caring for the crews of his ships. The captain had explained the distinction clearly to Rysn, in the same breath that she'd forbidden Rysn from *ever* asking again.

Rysn could order the ship to a destination, but she could not steer it. It was a distinction she'd never understood. And it meant that despite what the papers said, the ship was not Rysn's. She owned it. She commanded it. But at least according to maritime tradition, it was not *hers*.

Tradition. Stronger than Soulcast wood. If only they could find a way to build ships directly out of *it*, they'd fear no wind or wave.

The captain, Drlwan, was a short woman with a sharp nose and unusually blonde hair. Rysn hadn't realized until recently that having female officers was odd in other navies. In the Thaylen navy, while the bulk of sailors were men—trained to work the ballistae and repel boarders—female captains were common. Plus both the quartermaster and the navigator were women by tradition.

On the *Wandersail*, the soldiers were led by Kstled, the ship's man-at-arms, who was the captain's brother. Both captain and man-at-arms bowed formally to Rysn as she was carried up to the quarterdeck. Nikli and his assistant carried her in her wheeled chair to her new station: a tall seat, bolted to the deck, with a sunshade. It was out of the way of the helm, but would give her an excellent view of both the main deck and the surrounding ocean.

"Any thoughts?" she asked Nikli.

"It looks great, Brightness," he said, rubbing his chin. "You might want a table at the side—or better, something with a flat top and drawers you can latch shut."

"That's a good idea," she said.

"We can move one of your nightstands from the cabin, if you want," he said. "Would only require some basic carpentry. We'll try not to bother you too much setting it up."

She nodded in thanks, then had him move her from the wheeled chair—which had a place to strap it down nearby—to the new station. This had a belt to hold her in place. The extra support would be welcome on the rolling ocean waves. The chair also had, by her request, some leg straps she could fasten to keep her legs in place during rough seas, though she didn't intend to use those during ordinary sailing.

Nikli stowed her chair as she did up the belt. The burly porter didn't say anything, but eyed the captain as she stepped over. He obviously didn't like the way Rysn was treated on board, though he hadn't said anything on the matter.

"Rebsk," the captain said, calling Rysn by her formal title. It meant "shipmaster" or "owner." "I formally welcome you on board."

"Thank you," Rysn said.

"I would like to suggest, now, that you remain at port," Drlwan said. "You are not needed on this mission."

Rysn felt an immediate burst of frustration. "Why would you think that, Captain?"

"Your job is to handle trade negotiations," Drlwan said. "This voyage will include no such need. It is a survey mission. It could be dangerous, and as such, it would be wise if you remained safe at port. We can relay our experiences to you via spanreed."

"Your concern for my well-being is commendable," Rysn said, controlling her voice with effort. "But *I* have been tasked with this mission, and I will see it through."

"Very well," the captain said. She left to return to her post; by tradition she needed no dismissal from Rysn. And she never waited for one.

Nikli stepped over, handing her Chiri-Chiri, who was dozing. "I don't think the captain cares a wink for your safety, Brightness," he said softly. "She simply doesn't like you."

"I agree," Rysn said, idly scratching Chiri-Chiri under the neck as she watched the captain chat with the man-at-arms.

"Do you think it's because of . . . the way you are?"

"Possibly," Rysn said. "But usually others are uncomfortable—or condescending—around people like me, not outright hostile. Not everything in people's interactions with me is related to my condition."

So what *was* the reason so many of the crew resented her? She wasn't certain she could stand another full trip constantly feeling their eyes on her.

"I hesitate to mention this," Nikli said, "but perhaps it would be better to delay the trip and look for another crew. That would give us more time to install the table for you, also."

Rysn shook her head. "I need to learn to work with this crew. They are made up of my babsk's most trusted and accomplished sailors. Plus, they trained on this ship. They were sailing it on test runs before it was formally commissioned."

Nikli nodded and withdrew to stand near the steps, waiting for her commands. Rysn continued scratching Chiri-Chiri, lost in thought. Below, Queen Navani's team arrived: two Windrunners, an ardent scribe, and a young Horneater woman—perhaps in her late teens or early twenties—who Rysn thought must be their servant. The sailors hailed them, and a few cheered.

"An odd reaction," Rysn mumbled. Though she'd made her seat high, the railing to midship still obscured some of her view. An unfortunately common experience for her. "I would not have expected cheering."

"It's always good to have a Windrunner or two nearby, Rebsk," the man-at-arms said, walking past. "I'd never turn down passage to one of them."

This war had proven how vulnerable ships were

to enemies who could fly. Large stones—dropped from very high—could sink even the strongest of ships. But that reaction, the excitement from the crew . . . was it covering something? Rysn had been trained to watch for overexcitement in a trade deal. Sometimes a person would try too hard to sell a product or idea. The way the sailors acted reminded her of that.

"Captain?" Rysn said, calling over Drlwan again. "What has happened? Why are the sailors on edge?"

"It's . . . nothing, Rebsk," the captain said.

Rysn narrowed her eyes. Though she hadn't thought it remarkable at first—as the captain could be a showy woman—Drlwan was outfitted today in her formal dress uniform. Stark white, glistening with medals. She also wore an intimidating tricorn hat, her eyebrows curled and dangling beneath it. Although she had retired from official military service, the navy and the merchant marine were really two sides to the same card; ranks and accolades were shared between the two.

Today, that uniform was a show of force. A symbol.

"Tell me anyway," Rysn said.

Drlwan sighed. "Ship's pet was found dead this morning."

The ship's pet was a skyeel, good for hunting rats. Rysn knew from her previous voyage that a lot of the crew had liked her.

"Bad omen," Kstled muttered from behind.

That caused Drlwan to glare at him. Modern Thaylens weren't as superstitious as their ancestors— or at least they weren't supposed to be. They were good Vorins these days. And the coming of the Voidbringers—whose ways and worship seemed uncomfortably close to the Passions and Thaylen pageantry—hadn't done the old religions any favors. Rysn herself had drifted away from such ways of thinking, trying to be more intentional about her beliefs.

At any rate, Thaylens formally ignored omens. It was on the books, you might say, that such things were nonsense. Yet tradition was powerful, and when out at sea, logicspren could seem distant things indeed.

"Having a Windrunner on board," Rysn said. "Good omen?"

Kstled nodded, eyebrows sleek and tucked behind his ears. "You could call it a ... replacement for the dead skyeel. A counter-omen to the one this morning."

"It's all nonsense," the captain said. "I have told

the crew many times that I won't *stand* for this kind of talk."

"Indeed, you are wise," Rysn said. "Tell me, have the crew been informed of our destination?"

"They have."

"And did any express concern?"

The captain sniffed. "They were instructed, prior to the briefing, that there would be *no* questioning or grumbling. Queen Fen herself sent a writ supporting this mission. So we are *committed*."

"I see," Rysn said. "Spread my will among the crew. Tell them that if any have misgivings about our destination, they may remain behind—with no punishment—and join us again when we return."

Drlwan drew her lips to a line. She didn't like it when Rysn gave orders about the crew, though it was within Rysn's rights. "Very well, Rebsk," Drlwan said, nodding to her brother. He bowed to Rysn and ran off to pass the word.

"This could delay the mission," the captain noted.

"Then so be it," Rysn said. "I know that the crew still feels uncertain about following me, considering my lack of experience."

"You were hand-picked by Vstim and given this ship as a mark of his favor. No sailor would speak out against you."

And that isn't exactly a contradiction of what I said, now is it, Captain?

In that moment, a thought occurred to her. She'd been seeing this entire experience—Vstim giving her the ship, her elevation to rebsk—through her own eyes. But she had been taught to look at interactions in a different way. What did the captain want? Why was she dissatisfied?

You thought the answer a moment ago, Rysn told herself. *This ship was commissioned long before it was given to you. It was sailed by this crew for months. And then . . .*

"Captain," Rysn said, "did you know Vstim was going to retire?"

"He . . . spoke of it to me. And others who served him."

"Yet he commissioned a new ship. An expensive one, the jewel of his fleet. The best any sea had known. He told you to train a crew, to practice sailing it."

"And?"

"You thought he was going to give it to you, didn't you?" Rysn said, softening her tone. "You didn't realize he was planning to give it to me."

The captain stiffened. "No sailor would *presume* that a man like Vstim would simply *give* them a ship."

"But he mentioned he was taking an investment

position, didn't he?" Rysn said. "He knew an appointment from the queen was going to come to him, and he wouldn't be able to continue his expeditions. So he prepared you all ahead of time. He always watches out for the people he employs."

The captain, not meeting Rysn's eyes, gave an almost imperceptible hint of a nod.

Storms, that's it. That's why. Rysn's sudden elevation, and her arrival on the ship as its new master, must have taken the entire crew by surprise. Vstim wouldn't have prepared them for that, not when he hadn't been certain Rysn would take the appointment.

All this day, Rysn had been thinking about how the ship wasn't truly hers. Drlwan must have spent the entire previous voyage thinking the same exact thing.

"Is that all you need from me, Rebsk?" the captain asked.

"Yes," Rysn said. "Thank you."

The captain walked off to watch as her brother gathered the crew to relay Rysn's order. Nikli, always trying to be helpful, brought her a cup of some orange wine, not intoxicating.

"You heard?" Rysn said.

"That they are spoiled children? Angry that someone would dare earn an appointment above them?"

"That is a shallow way of thinking of it, Nikli," Rysn said, sipping the wine.

"I'm . . . sorry, Brightness. I'm merely trying to show you support."

"You can support me without denigrating others," Rysn said. "Think instead of how they must feel. You're new to my employ, so you might not know my reputation."

"I've heard you were a difficult apprentice."

"Difficult?" Rysn said, smiling. "*I* was a spoiled child, Nikli. I complained about every expedition I went on, despite being shown the very best treatment by my master—one of the most renowned traders in the nation. The sailors who served Vstim would have seen firsthand the type of person I was then. Even if none of these did, they'd have heard."

"Everyone acts a little entitled when young."

"True," Rysn said, "but you still wouldn't be happy when that entitled youth was given the ship you thought would be yours." She scratched Chiri-Chiri under the neck some more, earning a few quiet, contented chirps.

"So . . . what do we do?" Nikli asked.

"I do what Vstim did," Rysn said. "Spend my life earning the trust of those around me. The captain likely thinks she could do the trademaster's job, but she'd find negotiations far more difficult than she assumes. Vstim trusts me for a reason. I simply have to show the crew, through my actions, that his trust is well placed."

"I don't know, Brightness," Nikli said. He turned to glance toward the crew gathered around the man-at-arms, who spoke to them loudly. "I think you're giving them too much benefit of the doubt. I know how these sailors treated me during our previous trip. They don't like me. I have odd tattoos, and I'm a foreigner. I tried talking to them, but . . ."

"A ship's crew is a family," Rysn said. "They can be hostile to outsiders. I've felt it too. But if you really want to feel like one of them, ask Flend—he's the man on day shift in the eel's nest—if he has ever seen a sailorspren."

"What will that do?" Nikli asked, frowning.

"It should make him start a little hazing ritual they often put new sailors through. They love pranking new hands with that old trick."

"Hazing," Nikli said. "Brightness . . . I find the idea distasteful. We shouldn't encourage such behavior."

"Perhaps," Rysn said. "At first I thought it was cruel. Then I heard about the *old* hazing rituals. They were often humiliating, sometimes dangerous. After talking to my babsk, I started to realize something. Sometimes you accept deals you don't want, because they're better than the alternative.

"In a perfect world, no one would get hazed. But when I read about attempts by the military to stamp the practice out, I learned that doing so caused more mishaps. Banning hazing made the sailors afraid of being discovered, but it didn't stop them from acting on the sly with no warning, making it *more* dangerous. So several far safer practices were encouraged, with the officers looking the other way."

"A compromise with morality," Nikli said.

"An imperfect solution for an imperfect world," Rysn said. "I won't force you, of course. But if you want to get to know the others, give my suggestion a try. Play along with their prank, and I'll increase your wages by whatever they bilk out of you—it won't be much. They know not to push it too far."

Nikli retreated, seeming thoughtful, as Kstled finally returned to the quarterdeck. The captain joined him as he reported to Rysn.

"Only three crewmembers took the offer, Rebsk," he said. "And I think we can sail without them. We carry a larger complement these days in case of attack, and those two Radiants will more than make up for three lost swords. Though Nlan, the cook, was among the ones who decided to leave."

"That presents a problem," Drlwan said.

"I thought so as well," Kstled said. "But the Radiants said one of their companions is an excellent cook. So we could use her."

"I think that will do," Rysn said. "Captain?"

"Crew is ready, Rebsk. At your word."

"We sail, then."

5

Even with the best winds, a trip all the way from Thaylenah to Aimia would take weeks. Fortunately, Rysn had plenty to occupy her. There were future trade deals to begin setting up, and communications from paralyzed people around the world to answer. Rysn sincerely hoped she'd someday get to meet these friendly letter-writers in person.

The ship sheltered in coves for highstorms and Everstorms, which let Rysn go briefly ashore to send letters via spanreed. Although the *Wandersail* had been built to survive storms, sailing during one was still something they would do only in an emergency.

As the days passed, Rysn tried to learn about the people on her ship—though her crew was difficult to engage. She now recognized their resentment as a form of empathy for their captain, who they felt should have been given the ship. But even without that, talking to them would have been awkward. She was their rebsk, more unapproachable than an officer. When she tried to engage them in conversation, they'd respond in noncommittal ways or grow quiet.

The Lopen did not have that particular problem.

He was *fascinating.* She'd imagined Radiants, and seen them from afar—but hadn't met many. The one she had the most experience with was the solemn, quiet man she'd visited to see if her legs could be healed. He'd explained to her that he couldn't heal wounds that were more than a few months old. He'd been aloof, despite his obvious compassion for her situation.

She'd watched Windrunners soar overhead, and imagined them as mighty warriors. Battlefield legends who inspired with bold actions, heroic deeds. Larger than life. As if cut from stone, sculpted like the statues in the temples of the Heralds in Thaylen City.

"Now," the Lopen said to her, prancing around her chair in circles on hands and knees, "you *gotta* have two hands to properly crawl. I came up with my own version, sure, when I had one hand. But it was more of a shuffle. See?" He moved to crawling with one hand, the other behind his back.

"That . . . looks very much like crawling to me, Radiant the Lopen," Rysn said.

"It's *different* though," the Lopen said. "I tell you, I missed being able to do it."

"You missed crawling?"

"Sure. I'd lay in bed and think, 'Lopen, you used to be a *majestic* crawler. These louts don't know how good they have it, being able to crawl whenever they want.'"

"I can't imagine that if I were restored to the use of my legs, I would wish to do something so silly as crawl around."

He flopped down onto the deck beside her chair, rolling over and looking up. "Yeah, maybe. But it's nice to make people laugh at you for something you do, and not something you can't control. You know?"

"I . . . Yes. I think I do."

The ship surged across a wave. The seas were moderately rough today, though no storm was predicted. Wavespren danced atop the tips of whited caps across a field of shimmering blue. Rysn sat at her customary station on the quarterdeck, far aft, tucked in the corner beneath her sunshade and securely strapped in. Nikli had been true to his word, and so she now had a nightstand to her right, bolted to the deck, with a latching cabinet where she could store books and writing materials.

The captain gave the seat a look every time she passed, and Rysn could feel what she was thinking. What an impractical location. Sitting here, Rysn was exposed to the wind and occasional sprays of seawater. Why not stay in her cabin, as Drlwan had suggested?

People said things like that with a straight face, while being hit by wind and sprays of seawater themselves, never seeing the hypocrisy. Rysn wanted to be up where she could be seen, where she could watch the horizon. She wanted to listen to the sounds of the sea—the sprays, the crashes, and the calls of the sailors as they worked.

Nearby, Queen Navani's scribe—a slender ardent named Rushu—knelt beside a box, where she tinkered with some fabrials. Though they were a few weeks into the trip, Rysn hadn't yet received her promised demonstration of those—though she hoped it would happen today.

"So . . ." the Lopen said in Alethi, still lying on his back near her seat and staring up at the clouds, "know any good no-legged Thaylen jokes?"

"None worth sharing."

"One-legged jokes seem easier," the Lopen said.

"What do you call a one-legged Thaylen? Lean? Nah, that's not close enough to a real name. Hmm . . ."

"Lopen," Rushu said as she worked, "you should not be tormenting Brightness Rysn with your prattling."

The Lopen nodded absently. Then his eyes opened wide. "Oh! Why was the no-legged Thaylen unhappy? Because she'd been de-feeted. Ha! Hey Huio, listen."

Rysn couldn't help smiling as he proceeded to tell the joke in Herdazian to his cousin: a squat bald man with a wide, round face and beefy arms. She thought, from her limited knowledge of the Herdazian language, he then had to explain the pun—completely spoiling the joke. Yet the way the Lopen spoke—with such enthusiasm, such insistence on being seen and not ignored—made her feel relaxed. Even encouraged.

His cousin, in contrast, was a quiet man. Curiously, Radiant Huio had spent most of the trip so far lending a hand with various shipboard duties. He could tie knots and work the rigging like he'd been born on a ship. Today, he simply nodded pleasantly at the Lopen's joke and continued working on the rope he'd been untangling. That was a lowly duty, usually assigned to a sailor who had slept in late, but here a Knight Radiant was doing it without being asked.

"Lopen," Rushu repeated, "that was *not* appropriate."

"It's all right, Ardent Rushu," Rysn said.

"You shouldn't have to listen to things like that, Brightness," the ardent said. "It's unseemly to make mockery of your ailment."

"The thing that's unseemly," the Lopen said, "is how people treat us sometimes. Rysn, they ever ask about how it happened? And then get angry if you don't want to discuss it?"

"All the time," she said. "Ash's eyes, they keep *poking* at me, like I'm a riddle that exists only to entertain them. Others get quiet around me, and awkward."

"Yeah. I used to hate how folks would pretend I was gonna break at any moment."

"Like some kind of fragile vase that will tip off the shelf if upset. They can't see me. They see the chair."

"They act so uncomfortable," the Lopen continued. "They don't want to look, and don't want to bring it up, but it hovers about the conversation like a storming spren. But if you have the right joke . . ."

"Brightness Rysn shouldn't have to crack jokes at her own expense in order to make other people comfortable with their personal insecurities."

"Yup, true," the Lopen said. "She *shouldn't* have to."

Rushu nodded curtly, as if she'd won the argument. But Rysn understood the tone in the Lopen's voice. She shouldn't have to do such things, but life was unfair, and so you controlled the situation as best you could. Strange, to find such wisdom in a man she'd initially dismissed as silly. She inspected him lying on the deck, and he raised a fist in a gesture of solidarity.

"Radiant the Lopen," Rysn said, ". . . um, what do you call a Thaylen who can't walk?"

"Not sure, gancha."

"Names. From afar."

He grinned widely.

"Of course," Rysn added, "I'd never stand for that sort of thing."

The Lopen about died from laughing. He called to his cousin again, translating the jokes. This time Huio chuckled.

Rushu huffed, but moved closer to Rysn, carrying a box of gemstones and wire cages. "All right, Brightness. I am sufficiently prepared to provide a demonstration."

"Knowing you, sella," Lopen said to her, "you were prepared yesterday, and the day before, and the day before that. What happened? Get distracted by wondering how fish breathe?"

"We know how fish breathe, Lopen," Rushu said,

setting out her equipment on Rysn's table. Then she blushed. "I . . . got distracted by reading a new report on a curious interaction between flamespren and logicspren. The most *interesting* things are being discovered. Apologies, Brightness. I'm prone to letting the days slip past me now and then. But here, I'm ready."

She handed Rysn a silvery hoop with half of a glowing ruby attached to the top. "Hold that out in front of you, your arm straight. Excellent, just like that."

Rushu stepped back and held up a similar hoop. "Now, twist the gemstone's housing to conjoin them."

Rysn did so. Rushu let go of her hoop, and it remained hanging in the air. The hoop in Rysn's hand felt slightly lighter than it had before conjoining them.

"You're likely aware of this application of rubies," Rushu said, stepping beneath the sunshade. "It's how we make spanreeds. Two halves of a ruby, containing two halves of the same spren, can be made to move in tandem with one another.

"Many people, however, aren't aware that gemstones can be paired in such a way as to make their movements *opposite* one another. Traditionally we've used amethysts for this, but rubies work as well—and we have an excess of those from the ranches at the Shattered Plains. Now, move your hoop around—but carefully, as the paired one might move differently from the way you anticipate."

Indeed, as Rysn moved her hoop down, the floating one rose upward. If she moved her hoop left, the other moved right. It seemed to be a perfect transposition.

"We've known about this for a while," Rushu explained. "Our current creations are more in *application* than *innovation*. We've spent months developing housings for fabrials that won't unduly stress the gemstones, and have begun creating lattices that allow a large number of them to work in conjunction.

"That is how we create flying platforms. Each has a lattice of rubies conjoined to another lattice that is set up in a convenient location, such as alongside a plateau with a steep cliff. We can lower the cliffside lattice, and in so doing raise the lattice on a distant battlefield and provide a platform for scouts or archers."

"But spanreeds don't work on ships that are sailing," Rysn said, moving her hoop around and watching its other half respond. "Why does this?"

"Well, the problem with spanreeds is that a ship is always rocking and moving," Rushu explained. "If you're holding one in your lap and writing, you might *feel* that you're being steady—but since the entire ship is moving so much, the reed on the other side will be wobbling around and surging up and down. We've found that there is simply too much motion to properly use spanreeds this way. However, right now both of these hoops are on the same ship. They rock together, move together."

"But when the ship goes down," Rysn said, pointing at the other ring, "shouldn't it go up?"

"Yes, theoretically," Rushu said. "But it doesn't. Only your movements affect it. We believe this has to do with the frame of reference, as applied to the person moving the hoop. Spren, it should be noted, have a curious relationship to our perception of them and their motions. *You* see both of these hoops in the same frame of reference, so they act together. It's why the motion and curve of the planet don't influence spanreeds.

"It's proven impossible for someone on a ship with a spanreed to see themselves in the same frame of reference as the person receiving the communication. Perhaps there is a way to train ourselves, but no one has discovered it. Indeed, even the size of the ship can influence these things. If you tried this experiment on a rowboat, for example, the results could be different."

That . . . didn't make much sense to Rysn. Still, it was evident that the ship's motion didn't affect the two hoops. They both moved with it, rather than one ring being left behind—or being sent hundreds of feet in the opposite direction as the ship sailed forward.

Fabrials. Her babsk had always been fascinated with' them. Perhaps that was something Rysn should have picked up from him.

"So how's this going to help?" the Lopen said, sitting up beside her seat. "Oh! We're going to stick those to her legs, and then have this *other* person walk around, and she'll be able to look like she's walking!"

"Er," Rushu said, "we were rather thinking of making her seat hover in the air."

"Oh," the Lopen said. "That makes way more sense." He seemed disappointed nonetheless.

Rysn shook her head. "I see why Brightness Navani was hesitant to make any promises. If we *were* to make a chair hover for me, it wouldn't do me much good, would it? The chair would have to be attached to a lattice of gemstones, and then if I wanted to move forward, someone would have to move that lattice. So I'd still need porters and carriers."

"Unfortunately, yes, Brightness," Rushu said.

Rysn tried not to let disappointment show on her

face. The world was becoming a place of wonders—men and women soared in the air, and ships were being built with lightning rods right in the masts. At times, everything felt like it was progressing at an insane pace.

Yet none of it seemed able to help her. The healing was amazing . . . as long as your wound was fresh. The fabrials were incredible . . . as long as you had manpower to operate them. She had let herself begin to dream of a hovering seat she could direct under her own power, without needing to be hauled around like a roll of sailcloth.

Be careful, she thought. *Don't sink back into that lethargy of inaction.* Life *was* better for her now. She'd learned to change her surroundings to suit her needs. She dressed herself every morning with ease, using the hooks. Plus she had her own ship! Well, she owned a ship. At any rate, this was better than sitting in a dull room doing accounts.

"Thank you for the demonstration, Ardent Rushu," she said. "The technology is fascinating, even if the application doesn't seem suited to my needs."

"Well, Brightness Navani did assign me a list of tests to run," Rushu said. "She gave some thought to how this might help you in your specific situation. Perhaps you'd like to get a view as grand as that of the eel's nest? We could send you soaring up high. Or perhaps we can fashion a little lift to raise and lower you to and from the quarterdeck? That can be managed with some counterweights and a crank that can be wound periodically by one of the sailors."

That seemed a pale offering compared to her dreams, but Rysn forced out a smile. "Thank you. I should like to be available for those experiments."

Rushu deactivated the hoops and returned them to her box, along with some other machinery—including several silvery sheets of metal of varying thickness. "Aluminum," she explained as Rysn peered inside. "It blocks spanreed communication, something we only recently discovered. Navani wants me to experiment with how thick the aluminum needs to be to function, and then see if it affects—in any way—how paired rubies react, or don't react, to natural ship movements. I even have some foil, to . . . Oh, I'm getting too technical, aren't I? Sorry. I have a tendency to do that."

She looked to Rysn, then to the Lopen, who was sitting and rubbing his chin.

"Wait," he said. "Back up. I need an explanation."

"Lopen," Rushu said, "I hardly think I can—"

"How *do* fish breathe?" he said.

Rysn smiled at the ardent's exasperation. Rushu

thought it was a joke, but the Lopen seemed genuinely interested as he pestered her for an explanation.

A sudden motion distracted Rysn as Kstled rushed up to the quarterdeck and whispered something to the captain, who had been chatting with the current helmsman. Rysn focused on them, on Kstled's worried face, and on the captain's immediate frown.

Would they remember to inform her, whatever it was? The captain gave an order, then started down the steps. Halfway down, she paused to glance at Rysn—and noticed that Rysn was looking directly at her.

So, the captain—seeming annoyed—walked back up and trotted over.

"What?" Rysn asked, anxious. "What is wrong?"

"Dark Soulcasting," the captain said. "And bad omens. You should probably see it in person, Rebsk."

6

Cord, the Horneater woman, dug her hand into the barrel, then pulled it out, letting thick grains of lavis dribble between her fingers. This revealed the worms; though they were generally the same color as the grain, they uncurled and writhed on the surface, then buried themselves again.

"All of the barrels?" Rysn asked.

"Each and every one," Kstled said, nodding for his sailors to open two more barrels.

"I came to get supplies for food," the Horneater woman said in thickly accented Alethi. "And discovered. They are . . . every one this thing."

Rysn watched, troubled, as the sailors demonstrated the presence of worms in the other barrels. She kept meaning to find time to chat with Cord, but the woman had been spending her time in the galley, helping feed the crew. That had reinforced Rysn's initial assumption that she was a servant. The Radiants, however, didn't treat Cord that way. So who was she, and why was she here?

"The grain has been cursed," Kstled muttered. "Dark Soulcasting, performed by evil Passions during the storm."

"Or," Rysn said, trying to keep a level head, "we simply bought some stock with dormant larvae hiding inside."

"We checked thoroughly," Kstled said. "We *always* check. And look, this first barrel was left over from our original stores, taken on in Thaylen City. This other one was from an early resupply, and *this* one we picked up only two days ago. All have worms now."

She caught the other two sailors nodding, muttering about dark Soulcasting. Wormy grain wasn't the worst thing—many a sailor had eaten such during a long trip. But the sudden appearance of worms so early after restocking, and infesting all their barrels? This would be seen as an omen.

It was an old thing, of Thaylen superstition. The Passions, it was said, changed the world. "Spontaneous genesis has been disproven multiple times, armsman," Rysn said to Kstled. "This didn't happen because there's some kind of dark Soulcaster aboard our ship."

"Maybe it happened because of our destination," he replied. "The men dream terrible dreams full of premonitions, and their dread Passion creates omens." The other sailors nodded again. Storms, with this, and with the death of the ship's pet the day before setting sail . . . well, Rysn herself almost believed.

She needed to turn this attitude around quickly. "Kstled, how much of the crew knows about this?"

"All of them, Rebsk," he replied, glancing toward the Horneater woman.

"My sorrows," Cord replied. "I did not know this thing was . . . he was bad. . . . I asked others. . . ."

"It is done," Rysn said, turning to Nikli. "To my cabin, quickly."

The tattooed porter, along with his assistant, quickly carried her up from the hold to the higher decks. Yes . . . Rysn could imagine the convenience of a small lift, working via fabrial.

When she reached her cabin, she found the Lopen waiting for her. "Something wrong, gancha?"

"Corrupted food stores," Rysn said. Nikli held her chair while his assistant opened the door. "I need to do something about it quickly."

"I could fly to one of our outposts," the Lopen

said, following into her cabin. "Lash some more grain into the air and bring it to us."

"A viable suggestion," Rysn said as Nikli set her at her desk. She immediately began digging through the notebooks in the bottom drawer. Chiri-Chiri lethargically peeked out of her box and chirped in concern. "However, I feel we need another solution."

She pulled out a specific notebook, then nodded to Nikli, who bowed and withdrew with his assistant to stand outside. The Lopen remained, lounging beside the door as it clicked closed. She glanced at him. He acted so relaxed all the time; he seemed easy to underestimate.

"This isn't about just our lack of food, gancha," he guessed.

"An astute observation," Rysn said, flipping through her notebook. "One of the biggest dangers at sea is letting your crew get away from you."

"Like that crew from the ghost ship," Lopen said, "who seem to have gotten away from *everyone* . . ."

"I wasn't referring to anything so dramatic," Rysn said. "But our situation could quickly turn dangerous if the crew starts to think I've brought them on a suicide mission."

It was one of the conundrums of maritime life. Sometimes good crews, well trained, would mutiny. Her babsk had talked about it, and she'd found herself reading story after story. Spending so long on the ocean, isolated, the crew's emotions fed off one another. Things that were irrational during brighter days started to seem reasonable. Emotions could take on a life of their own, like spren, and suddenly good crews would become hysterical.

Your best defenses were discipline and swift action. She searched her notebook for notes from a specific trading expedition she'd taken with Vstim several years ago. She'd been a brat back then—but at least she'd been the kind of brat who wrote about how annoyed she was.

There, she thought, finding the entries. An expedition into the wilderness of Hexi. Vstim had purchased wormy grain out of Triax for mere chips, and she'd thought him insane. Who *bought* grain with worms in it?

But as with all things he'd done, there'd been an explicit lesson in Vstim's actions. Trade wasn't only about buying things and selling them, he'd reinforced to her time and time again. It was about finding a need that wasn't being fulfilled. It was a kind of Soulcasting: taking scraps and transforming them into the brightest of gemstones. He'd made her write down a list of locations. . . .

"Fetch the captain for me," Rysn said absently, unrolling one of her maps.

She didn't realize until after he'd gone that she'd given an order to a Knight Radiant. Would he be insulted? But when the Lopen returned with Drlwan, he didn't seem the least bit offended. Merely curious as he looked over her shoulder at the map.

"Rebsk?" the captain asked.

"We need to take a short detour," Rysn said, pointing at the map.

Rysn made certain the entire crew was on deck to watch as she invited the Hexi nomads on board. A quiet folk, uninterested in the politics of the world, they kept their hair in braids and smelled faintly of the animals they kept as sacred beasts. Their priestly class did not eat flesh, as they'd taken oaths forbidding it—but they considered grubs and insects to be plant, not animal.

They were one of six groups Vstim had made her write down as people to whom she could sell wormy grain. To initiate the trade, Rysn read off the phrases that Vstim had required her to record. The nomads sifted through the grain and found it to be good, barely eaten by the worms—which were plump and fat.

Careful not to take advantage, Rysn negotiated briefly, but firmly. The end result was a large stock of jerky, made by the nomads from the dead of their animals and kept specifically for trades like this.

The blankets—given as a gift to Rysn, with the phrase "For an Honored" because of her respectful language—would sell for a good bit as well. The nomads left with the barrels of grain, singing their farewell.

"They actually bought *worm-filled* grain," the captain said, scratching her head. "I'll admit, Rebsk, I hadn't believed you until just now."

"Vstim never brought you here, I take it," Rysn said.

"Ah. This did smell of one of his schemes. I wonder why this isn't common knowledge. This place should be swarming with traders trying to offload their old grain for profit."

"You'd think that," Rysn said, "but that's not what I learned from Vstim. The Hexi tribes must be approached carefully, and their language is difficult to learn. Act arrogant, and you'll turn them away. Plus, the grain needs to be fresh good grain—though with worms. They won't buy something that has festered and is full of decayspren."

"Still," the captain said.

And she was right. This *was* a mostly untapped market. But who wanted to trade wormy grain when there were fine rugs and jewelry to show off? Who wanted to visit the Hexi wilderness when the grand bazaars of Marat were so close?

Only someone who understood need and the true soul of a trader. *Thank you, Babsk,* she thought as she surveyed her crew and saw far fewer anxiety-spren than before. This had mollified them. These last few days had been tense, but the crew were more jovial as they returned to their stations.

Rysn had, hopefully, inverted the omen. That was the traditional way to disperse such a thing: to derive a good turn from it. To those who followed the Passions, this showed that fate was on your side, even when an omen tried to darken the way. You could always defeat gloomy Passions with optimism and determination. Even the worst highstorm dropped fresh water.

It was all nonsense, she'd come to believe—but it was the most intriguing kind because of the underlying truth. Omens weren't real. But the way people reacted to them was *very* real. Inverting that was all about perspective. Like how a barrel full of worms was worthless or of great value, depending on your perspective.

Nikli picked her up at her request; for simple transfers like this, he brought her in a cradle-carry rather than using his sling, which she could sit in. As he walked toward the quarterdeck, a couple of the sailors waved to him and called out a good-natured joke, at which Nikli smiled.

"It worked, I see," she said as he deposited her in her seat beneath the sunshade. "You seem to have made a few friends on board."

"I . . ." Nikli bowed his head. "I guess I shouldn't have doubted. Yes, Brightness. They eat with me now, ask about my homeland. They are not so prejudiced as I thought."

"They are and they aren't," she said. "As I said, sailors on a ship can be a tight-knit group. But these here on the *Wandersail* chose this duty, preferring long-distance voyages that take them new places. They're not the type to dislike someone solely because he looks a little different—at least, no more than they distrust anyone else who isn't part of their ship family. You merely needed to join that family."

Nikli knelt beside her chair as she buckled herself in. "You are also different from what I expected, Brightness. I thought working for a merchant would involve . . . Well, thank you. For the way you treated those nomads earlier, and the way you treat me. For your wisdom."

"I wish it were my wisdom, Nikli," Rysn said. "I was trained very well by a teacher I didn't deserve, and can never live up to."

"Brightness," Nikli said, "you seem to be doing a fine job, in my estimation."

She appreciated the words, but now that she

knew how the crew felt about her, she found it more difficult to quiet the voice inside. The one that whispered she didn't deserve to own this ship. She hadn't earned this station. She hadn't made the money, proven her acumen, or worked her way up to being a shipmaster. Everything Rysn possessed, she had been given.

There was an uncomfortable truth to the way the captain regarded her. Rysn *was* untested. She *was* undeserving. Even victories like the one she'd accomplished today had been achieved by leaning on Vstim and his lessons. She wouldn't stop doing that, of course. Ignoring what she'd been taught out of some kind of petulant spite was exactly the kind of thing the youthful her would have done.

That voice persisted anyway.

"You know," Nikli said, still kneeling beside her chair and scanning the ship, "I have this strange, perhaps selfish piece inside me that didn't *want* the crew to like me. It was easier to think of them all as bigots." He looked down at the deck. "That was small of me."

"No, just human of you," Rysn said. "You know, you still owe me the story of why you left your homeland. Don't think I've forgotten."

"It isn't a great story, Brightness," he said. "We

are a small village, my people. Not much of interest about us."

"I'd like to hear it anyway."

Nikli thought for a moment. Rysn had traveled quite a bit of the world, and she'd never seen tattoos like his—they had been inked over some kind of scar tissue, as if his skin had been carved, allowed to heal, then overlaid with the white tattoos.

"I was betrayed," he finally said, "by someone I trusted. Soon after, one of us was needed to go to Thaylenah—my people, though small, like to know what is happening in the great nations of the world. I volunteered. So I wouldn't have to be around the one who had treated me so."

That only raised more questions in her mind. She didn't press him. It didn't feel right.

"Did your master have any wisdom to share about traitors?" Nikli asked. "About how to deal with someone you trust who turns against you?"

"Vstim said to always read contracts with friends an extra time," Rysn said softly.

"That's it?"

"I asked him, on another occasion, to explain. He said, 'Rysn, being cheated is a terrible feeling. Being cheated by someone you love is worse. Discovering such a deception is like finding yourself in a deep dark ocean with nothing around you but formless shadows of things you once thought you understood and enjoyed. It is painful beyond explanation. But that is *never* a reason to pretend it can't happen. So read those contracts again. Just in case.'"

Nikli grunted. "That's . . . a different kind of wisdom than I'd anticipated. I thought maybe this man lived purely a life of charity."

"Vstim is good and honest," Rysn said. "But you don't get a reputation for either without some people seeing your nature as an opportunity." He'd warned her of that fact too, and she'd often wondered what specific experiences had taught him the painful lessons. He'd never shared the details.

"Brightness," Nikli said. "I hesitate to say this, but . . . I think you should know. I am the type of person many ignore, and I listen well. I overhear things. I think . . . Brightness, I think the Radiants and their friends are hiding things from you."

"Why would they do that?" Rysn asked.

"I don't know. But they were talking, and the ardent told one of them to quiet down, lest the crew— or you—overhear. Something to do with the mission. That's all I heard. But I do feel I should point out that the Horneater was the first to discover the worms. And the Radiants still haven't come up with a good explanation for why she's on this voyage."

"What are you implying?" Rysn said.

"No implication. Merely sharing what I heard."

"I think we can trust the Knights Radiant," Rysn said.

"I'm sure people also thought that two thousand years ago," Nikli said. Then he sighed and stood up. "But I probably shouldn't have said anything. I need to go to the head, but I'll return soon, Brightness."

Rysn discarded the idea that the Knights Radiant had planted those worms. But there *were* questions that itched at her. How had those worms appeared so suddenly? And what had killed the ship's pet? Rysn realized she hadn't asked.

But as the ship set out, she considered. She obviously wouldn't be the only one who understood that omens—despite being nonsense—could have powerful effects on the people who observed them. If someone wanted to interfere with this mission, a few well-placed omens would be an excellent way.

Be careful about jumping to conclusions, she told herself. The solution was to watch.

Because if she was right, another "omen" would soon arrive.

Nikli stepped into the head, locked the door, and turned off the body's sense of smell to avoid being bombarded by the odor of this place. Nikli held up this body's hand and made a fist, pleased by how long the form held. But now Nikli relaxed, and the seams in the body's skin split, letting cool air reach into its squirming insides—which shivered, relieved to finally be allowed free motion after keeping tight for so long.

At the same time, Nikli closed the body's most obvious set of eyes—its human eyes, which were actually functional, something Nikli was proud of. Most Sleepless used prop eyes. That caused their sight lines to be off, easier to notice.

With the body's eyes closed, it was easier to feel the distant pieces of the self. Spread all across Roshar. And Nikli could make them buzz, communicating with the others, speaking directly from mind to mind as its buzzes were interpreted by hordelings bred specifically for the purpose.

We, Nikli sent to the others, *have a problem.*

Indeed we do, Nikliasorm, sent Alalhawithador, who had a low, angry buzz. *They aren't responding to your encouragements to turn back. You have failed. Other measures will be required.*

The problem is not that, Nikli sent. *The problem is that I am coming to like them.*

This is not unexpected, Yelamaiszin sent. It had a smooth, calming buzz. It was First, the oldest of the swarms on Roshar. Nikli was the Twenty-Fourth, youngest of them. *I like the Bondsmith, for example, though I know he will destroy us.*

He will not, Zyardil sent. Its buzz was punctuated and sharp. *He has made the decision of Honor.*

That is why he will *destroy us,* Yelamaiszin replied. *He is more dangerous now, not less.*

This is a different argument, said Alalhawith-ador, who was Third—a swarm almost as old as Yelamaiszin. *You like these humans, Nikliasorm. That is good. We are so bad at imitating them, and you learn well from your travels. More of us should spend time studying humans, to become like them.*

Plus, Yelamaiszin said, *we should have compassion for those we must cull. It is good you like the humans.*

Must we cull them though? Nikli replied.

Humans are a fire that must be contained, Yela-maiszin said with its calm buzz. *You are young. You were not yet Separated during the scouring.*

I would like to try again to ward them away, Nikli sent.

This is a mess, said Alalhawithador, the angriest of the swarms. *It should not have gone this far. You should have killed them before this.*

They should not have found the ship, Zyardil sent. *This would all be contained if it hadn't been discovered.*

It was sent to sink, Alalhawithador replied. *It could not have survived storms without help. Its discovery is no coincidence.*

Arclomedarian crosses us again, said Yelamaiszin, the First. *It meddles more and more. It has met with these new Radiants.*

Are we certain it was wrong to do so? Nikli asked. *Perhaps that was the wise move.*

You are young, Yelamaiszin sent, calm and sure. *Youth is beneficial in some ways. You learn faster than us, for example.* Nikli could imitate humans better than the others. When the swarm that had become Nikli had been Separated, it had already contained hordelings evolved for this subterfuge. Nikli had further evolved them, and was now certain that the body didn't need the tattoos to cover the seams in its skin.

Arclomedarian is dangerous, Nikli sent. *I can see this. But it is not as dangerous as the true traitors.*

Both are equally dangerous, Yelamaiszin sent. *Trust us. You do not bear the scars of memory older swarms do.*

We must listen to the youthful, Zyardil snapped. *They are not set in their ways! The humans that come this time are not pirates, First, looking only for lucre. They are more persistent. If we kill them, there will be more.*

My plan is the best, Alalhawithador sent with a feisty set of buzzing noises. *Let them breach the storm.*

No, Yelamaiszin said. *No, we must prevent that.*

At this point of conflict, the question was sent to all of the swarms—all twenty that still accepted the leadership of the First—to ask. Was it time to sink the human ship?

The responses were tallied. It was a stalemate, they decided. Half wanted to let the humans reach the storm—where they would either fall to the winds or enter the realm of the Sleepless. Half wanted to kill them immediately, before the storm. Several, like Nikli, abstained from the vote.

Nikli's own swarm buzzed with relief and satisfaction at the uncertainty in the others. This was an opening.

I would like to try one more time to ward them off, Nikli repeated. *I have an idea that I believe will work, but I will need help.*

This was sent to another vote, and Nikli's bodies— the distant ones, not on the ship—all vibrated with anticipation.

Yes, the vote came. Yes, Nikli should be allowed to try again.

It hurts us to kill Radiants, let alone one of the Sighted, said Yelamaiszin, the First. *You may try this plan. If it fails, however, I will hold another vote—and you must be willing to take more drastic measures.*

7

"Does something about the crew seem strange
to you?" Lopen asked as he lounged in the air
about three feet off the deck, hands behind his head,
floating beside Cord.

The sturdy Horneater was mixing something
that smelled good. It was pungent with the spices that
he associated with Rock's cooking—which wasn't
spicy hot, just ... full of other flavors. Interesting
ones. This dish, though, also had an oceany scent she
said came from seaweed. Who ate weeds? Weren't
her people supposed to eat shells?

"Strange?" she asked Lopen. "Crew?"

"Yeah. Strange." He watched several of the sailors go tromping past, and they kept shooting him
looks. Rua trailed after them in the air, invisible to

everyone but Lopen and Cord, who, like her father, could see all spren.

"You all strange," she admitted. Each word was hesitant, but her Alethi was progressing well.

"So long as I'm the strangest," Lopen said. "It's, sure, one of my more endearing traits."

"You are . . . very strange."

"Excellent."

"Very *much* strange."

"Says the woman who likes to munch on weeds," Lopen said. "That's not food, misra, it's what food eats." He frowned as several more sailors passed by, and a couple made strange Thaylen gestures toward him. "See that! They *cheered* when we came on board. Now they've gotten all weird."

Things had been better after the stop in Hexi to sell that grain, and Lopen approved of the jerky. But now, as they were reaching the halfway point in their journey, everything had gotten odd. There was a strange tone to every interaction, and he couldn't quite figure out what it meant.

He glanced up as Huio streaked in overhead, then lowered himself down to the deck. He delivered a letter to Cord—from her parents, most likely—and tucked a few others into the inner pocket of his uniform coat for Rysn, who had asked him to visit a nearby island and receive letters for the day.

"Thank you," Cord said to Huio, lifting up the letter. "Is happiness to hold him."

"Welcome," Huio said. "Was easy. Not problem."

Watching them interact in Alethi was amusing. Why were there so many languages, and why didn't everyone just learn Herdazian? It was a great language. It had names for all the different kinds of cousins.

"Huio," Lopen said in Alethi, so as to not leave Cord out, "has the crew been treating you strangely?"

"No," he said. "Um, no sure?"

"Not sure?" Lopen said.

"Yes. Not sure." He set down his satchel, which carried spanreeds and other equipment. He reached in and brought out the small box of aluminum plates and foils that Rushu had sent with him, to use in some experiments trying to communicate back to her on the ship. "You know this?" Huio asked of them.

"Aluminum," Lopen said, still floating above the deck a few feet. "Yeah, it's weird stuff. Can block a Shardblade, Rua tells me, if it's thick enough. They get it from Soulcasting, though only a few can make it, so it's pretty rare."

"Can get from trade," Cord said. "In Peaks. We trade."

"Trade?" Huio said. "Who trade?"

"People in spren world," Cord said.

Huio cocked his head, rubbing his chin.

"He is strange metal," Cord said. "Does strange things to spren."

"Strange," Huio agreed. He packed up the materials in his satchel and went wandering off. Hopefully he'd deliver them to Rushu, rather than playing with them. Huio sometimes got himself into trouble that way.

"Your people, Cord," Lopen said, turning in the air like he was lounging on a sofa. "They have water up in those peaks. How? It's cold, right?"

"Cold away from town," she said. "Warm near town."

"Huh. That sounds interesting."

"He is." She smiled. "I love him, our land. Didn't want leave. Had leave with Mother. To find Father."

"You could return, if you wanted," Lopen said. "Wouldn't take much to have a Windrunner fly you."

"Yes," she said. "But now, out here, he is dangerous. Good dangerous. I not wish to go. Too love of home, yes? But now that I see him, I cannot return. Not with danger here, for people. Danger that will go my home." She turned from her mashing and looked across the ocean. "I was scared of places not home. And now . . . I find things that make scared are also things that make interesting. I like dangerous things. I did not know this."

Lopen nodded. What an interesting way to see the world. Mostly he enjoyed listening—he liked the way Cord's accent made a cadence of her words, and the way she drew out some vowel sounds. Plus she was tall, and tall women were best. He'd been very curious to find she was only a few years younger than he was. He hadn't expected that.

Alas, he had stuck Huio to the wall for her on three separate occasions, and Cord had not seemed to find it impressive. He'd also cooked her chouta, but she already made it better than he did. Next he'd have to find a way to show her how good he was at cards.

"That's interesting," he said. "You like things you're afraid of?"

"Yes. But I did not realize this thing. Afraid thing. Yes?"

"You didn't realize that something fearsome, something different, could be so intoxicating. I think I get what you're saying." He thought for a moment, drinking the Light from a big garnet gemstone. The others called him silly, but he thought the different colors *tasted* different.

He eyed Cord. Was she impressed by how casually he floated? No way to know without pointing it out, which was the *opposite* of being casual. So he put his hands behind his head, and thought more about what she'd said.

"Cord," he said, "your father. Is he really in danger because of what he did? Saving Kaladin? Killing Amaram?"

It had been several months since the event, and Kaladin had persuaded Rock to remain in Urithiru for the time being. Mostly to give his family a season to rest from their extended trip. However, that wouldn't last forever. Rock was increasingly intent on returning to his homeland to face judgment.

"Yes," Cord said softly. "But because of him. His doing. His wanting."

"He made the choice to help Kaladin," Lopen said, "but he didn't choose his birth order."

"But his choice to go back. His choice to ask for . . . I do not know word. Ask for choice?"

"Judgment?"

"Yes, maybe." She smiled at him. "Do not afraid for my father, Lopen. He will choose his choice. If he must go home, I will stay. And Gift will stay. We will do his work. We will see for him."

"See," Lopen said. "See spren, you mean?"

She nodded.

"Are there any around now?" Lopen asked.

"Rua," she said, pointing as Lopen's spren came darting over in the shape of a fanciful flying ship. "And Caelinora." Huio's spren. She rarely appeared to Lopen.

"Windspren in the air, wavespren in the water. Anxiety-spren trailing the ship, almost unseeable. And . . ." She shook her head.

"And what?" Lopen asked.

"Odd things. Good gods, but uncommon. *Apali-ki'tokoa'a.*" She struggled to find the right words, then took out a piece of paper—she often carried some—and did a quick sketch.

"A luckspren," Lopen said, recognizing the arrowhead shape.

"Five," she said. "Was none. Then was three. Then four. More each few day."

Huh. Well, he was glad she was watching—she'd been hesitant to come on the trip, as she hadn't thought she would be of any use. He'd encouraged her, since he knew she wanted to see the world more. And here she was, seeing interesting spren.

"I don't know if luckspren are something to be worried about," he said, "but I'll have Rushu report it anyway. Queen Jasnah or one of the others might think something of them."

Cord nodded, so he cut his Lashing. That made him land on the deck with a thump, a little harder than he'd intended. He patted the wood and grinned, feeling foolish. Too bad Huio hadn't been watching. He'd have enjoyed that.

Lopen jogged off to find his cousin—who, as Lopen had feared, was in their cabin poking at Ardent Rushu's spanreeds. He appeared to have completely disassembled one.

"Lopen," Huio said in Herdazian. "This aluminum has fascinating properties; I believe the captive spren are reacting to its presence, almost like prey react to a predator. When I touch this foil to the stone, they push to the other side of their confines. I hypothesize that the aluminum interferes with their ability to sense not only my thoughts of them, but the thoughts of their conjoined half."

"You know, cuz," Lopen said in the same language, "those spanreeds are *way* more valuable than the locks you used to break apart. You could get into trouble."

"Perhaps," Huio said, tinkering with a small screwdriver to undo part of the gemstone's housing, "but I am certain I can reassemble it. The ardent-lady will be completely unaware of my investigation."

Lopen flopped down on his bunk. He'd asked for a hammock, like the crew used, but they'd acted like he was crazy. Apparently beds were in short supply on a ship. Which made sense. Everyone else got storming *hammocks*! Who'd want a bed?

"Something feels wrong about this entire mission," Lopen said.

"You're merely bored, younger-cousin," Huio said,

"because the crew are too busy with their work to be entertained by your unruly antics."

"Nah, it's not that," Lopen said, staring at the ceiling. "And maybe it's not even this trip. Things are just . . . off lately, you know?"

"Oddly—though everyone always expects me to be able to decipher what you're saying—I find myself at a loss most of the time. And not only when you're speaking in Alethi. Fortunately, you're usually around to explain. At length. With lots of adjectives."

"You know, Cord is getting pretty good with Alethi."

"Good for her. Maybe she can learn Herdazian next, and then someone will finally *interpret* for me when I'm lost."

"You'll pick it up eventually, older-cousin," Lopen said. "You're, sure, the smartest person in our family."

Huio grunted. His inability with the Alethi language was a sore spot with him. It didn't click in his head, he said. Years of trying, and he hadn't made much progress. But that was all right. It had taken Lopen, sure, *years* to learn how to grow an arm back after he lost one.

So what *was* bothering Lopen? Was it the things Cord had said? He took his rubber ball out of his pocket and practiced infusing it, then sticking it to the ceiling, then catching it again when it dropped.

The Voidbringers had come back. But they weren't *actually* the Voidbringers. They were just parshmen, but different. And the war had started, like in the old stories. There was a new storm, and the world had basically ended. It all seemed so *intense*.

But in reality, it was so storming slow.

They'd been fighting for months and months, and lately it seemed like they were making less progress than Huio on his Alethi. Kill some of those new singers with the strange powers—they were called Fused—and they'd get reborn. Fight and fight and fight, and maybe capture, sure, a few dozen feet of ground. What a party. Do that for a million centuries, and maybe they'd have an entire kingdom.

Shouldn't the end of the storming world be more . . . dramatic? The war against the invaders felt depressingly like the war over the Shattered Plains. Sure, Lopen kept an upbeat attitude. That helped everyone. But he couldn't help making the comparison in his head.

His side were the good guys. The Radiants. Urithiru. All of it. He'd decided they were, despite bad choices by some of the Radiants in the past.

But he thought about the Shattered Plains. And how *stupid* that battle had been, stretching all those years. How many good people had it killed? He couldn't help worrying they were now headed into a mire of cremwater just as bad, if not worse.

"I wish," he said, "that this ship could move faster. I wish we could be *doing* things. This is taking too long."

"*I'm* doing things," Huio said. He turned around in his seat at the desk, holding up the repaired spanreed. "See? It has been returned identically to its previous state."

"Yeah? Does it still write?"

Huio made a few circular scribbles on a piece of paper from the satchel. The conjoined spanreed, in turn, jerked across the paper in a single line, back and forth.

"Uh . . ." Huio said.

"You person-who-has-rotten-fruit-for-a-head!" Lopen said, jumping to his feet. "You broke it."

"Uh . . ." Huio repeated, then made another scribble. The pen reacted as before, moving left and right on the page in accordance with his motions, but it didn't go up or down on the page when he moved his pen to the top or bottom. "Huh."

"Great," Lopen said. "Now I'm going to have to tell boss ardent-lady. And she will say, 'Lopen, I can see that you are very careful, and often not breaking things, but I'd still rather your older-cousin *not* have rotten fruit inside his skull instead of brains.' And I'll agree."

"They have a ton of these things," Huio said. "There's at least, sure, twenty pairs in the storage they sent us. I doubt it will be an exceeding burden if one is malfunctioning." He scribbled again. Same result. "Maybe I could—"

"Try to repair it?" Lopen said, skeptical. "I suppose. You're, sure, super smart. But . . ."

"But I'd probably break it further." Huio sighed. "I thought I had it figured out, younger-cousin. They don't seem even as complicated as a clock."

"And how many of *those* have you managed to put together correctly after taking them apart?"

"There was that once . . ." Huio said.

Lopen met his eyes, then they shared a grin.

Huio slapped him on the arm. "Return those to the ardent-lady. Tell her I will pay for the broken reed, if it's a problem. It will have to be next month though."

Lopen nodded. Both of them, along with Punio, gave most of their Radiant stipend to the family for helping out with the poorer cousins. A big chunk went to Rod's family. Radiants were paid well, but there were a lot of cousins who needed help. It was their way—when Lopen had been the poor one, they'd always helped him.

Lopen walked out onto the deck, proud of how well he'd adapted to the swaying of the ship. However, he stopped as he noticed a large group of sailors congregating on the left side of the ship. The, uh, starboard side? He wandered over, and then Lashed himself upward to see over their heads.

Something was floating in the water nearby. Something large. And something that was very, very dead.

8

Rysn felt a sinking sense of dread as Nikli carried her to the side of the ship. The sailors had bunched up here, attended by anxietyspren—like twisting black crosses—and a few globs of fearspren. They made way for Rysn, and Plamry—Nikli's Thaylen assistant—hurried forward and set down a high stool for her. She gripped the rail to steady herself as Nikli placed her on the stool, then she nodded for him to retreat.

That made room for the captain to step up and stand beside her. Sitting there, Rysn could peer over the side of the ship to see what the others had been whispering about: a dead santhid. A decaying shell and husk, flipped over on its side, its whited eye staring toward the sky. It was enormous, nearly a third as long as the ship itself.

The large marine creatures were incredibly rare. She had believed them extinct, but had enjoyed stories from her babsk about them. They supposedly rescued drowning sailors, or trailed ships for days, improving the moods of those on board. More spren than animal, they were somehow able to magnify peace and confidence.

Likely that was as much fancy as the Passions. But no sailor she'd ever met would speak ill of santhidyn, and meeting one was among the best omens in the ocean. She didn't need to ask to know what finding a *dead* one would do to the mood of her crew.

The sailors sensed this was coming, she thought. *They've been on edge these last few days, waiting.* Perhaps, like Rysn, they'd noticed the pattern—and had expected a third, worst omen. To them, this would be proof the trip was cursed.

And, as she looked down at that large unnatural corpse—she found herself questioning. Sure, omens *seemed* like nonsense. But she'd assumed the Voidbringers were only stories, and they'd returned. Her mother had always laughed at the idea of Lost Radiants wandering the storms as spirits, but now she had two Radiants on her ship. Who was Rysn to say what was fact and what was myth?

No, she thought. *There must be another explanation. Could someone have planted this?*

She'd been expecting a third omen like the grain or the dead pet. Something a person could achieve in secret. But this . . . this went far beyond such simple plots. Did she really think someone hiding among her crew had managed to find a near-mythical creature, kill it, and deposit it in the ocean without raising suspicion?

No one has to have planted it, she told herself firmly. *This could still be a random unlucky event.*

She glanced down again, and *swore* that oversized eye was looking at her. Seeing right through her, even in death. As decaying chunks of the santhid began to float off from the main body, she felt as if she were being *watched*. And she became suddenly aware of the crowding sailors' mood. Dark. Too quiet. No mentions of what a bad omen this was. They already knew. There was nothing more to say.

"We'll be turning back after *this*," said Alstben, a tall sailor who liked to spike his eyebrows. He looked at Rysn. "No way we continue."

Storms. It wasn't a question. Rysn searched for support from the captain, but Drlwan folded her arms and didn't contradict the sailor. Doing so would likely invite mutiny. This crew was probably too loyal to do such a thing as kill their captain, but . . . well, if the *Wandersail* returned to dock with its captain, armsman, and owner locked up because they'd "gone mad," who would blame the crew? Particularly after an omen as sure as a dead santhid.

Rysn nearly gave the order. She knew when a trade deal was mired in crem, when it was better to walk away with your goods than try to force an accommodation.

And yet. That meant giving in to the superstitions. And someone *was* trying to spook her crew, even if this specific event was random. Turning back meant giving in to whoever that was.

Most importantly, turning back meant giving up on helping Chiri-Chiri. Sometimes the trade was too important to walk away from. Sometimes you *had* to negotiate from a position of weakness.

"Why is it floating?" Rysn asked the sailors. "Shouldn't it have sunk after it died?"

"Not necessarily," Kstled said, emerging from the rear of the crowd. "I've passed a ship lost to ramming before. Days later, bloated corpses still floated in the water, nibbled at from below by fish."

"But something this big?" Rysn asked. "With that shell?"

"Greatshell corpses can float," another sailor said. "Pieces of them, after they're dead. I've seen it."

Damnation. Rysn didn't know enough to keep pushing on this line of reasoning. Yet it seemed so unlikely that they had randomly run across this right in their path. Maybe there was another option. Maybe it wasn't one person working to undermine her mission, but a larger organization. The enemy had Fused, creatures with powers like Radiants. This could be a Lightweaving, or a Soulcast dummy, or any number of things.

She didn't want to give up. Not without more time to think, and maybe a chance to inspect this corpse. So, she took a deep breath. Sometimes a negotiation was all about attitude.

"Very well," she said. "Let us do what is right, then. Get the boarding hooks and get ready to tow that corpse."

"Tow it?" one of the sailors asked. "Surely we're not going to try to *profit* by selling the shell?"

"Of course not," Rysn said. "What kind of craven do you think I am? We're going to give the creature a proper funeral. And if it seems the beast's will, we will keep the shell for the luck it represents and present it to the queen. It is fortunate we happened along, so the body might be burned as befits the creature's majesty."

". . . Fortunate?" Kstled asked.

"Yes," Rysn said. She had trained herself not to feel intimidated when seated among a crowd of standing people, but it was difficult not to feel her old insecurities as so many of them turned to stare down at her, skeptical—even angry.

Attitude, she reminded herself. *You will never sell anything if you don't believe it's worth the asking price.*

"Someone killed this poor thing," Rysn continued. "Look at those gouges on the side of the corpse."

"Bad luck," a sailor said. "*Extremely* bad luck to kill a santhid."

"Which we did *not* do," Rysn said. "Someone *else* did, and incurred the bad luck. *We* are lucky to have found the creature so we can witness what was done to it—and see the body cared for."

"We shouldn't touch a santhid corpse," said Kstled, folding his arms.

"I've seen their shells hung proudly in Thaylen City," Rysn said. "There's one at the naval academy!"

"Those weren't killed by malice," Kstled said. "Besides, they washed up on the shore. Found their way there."

"Like *this one,*" Rysn said, "made its way to *us,* here. How vast is the ocean? And yet *we* happen across this relatively small body? The santhid's soul undoubtedly led us here so we could witness and care for the corpse." She pondered, as if thinking of it for the first time. "This is a *good* omen. It came to us intentionally. A sign that we are trusted."

She hid the uncertainty she felt, knowing her argument was full of holes and sinking fast. She decried superstition, but now she relied upon it to make this argument?

Nevertheless, it seemed to work. A few sailors nodded. That was the thing about omens—they were made up. Imagined signals of something nebulous. So why not make them up to be something positive?

"We always consider it a good sign when one washes up on shore," a man said. "Why is this different?"

"We need to spread the word," said another, "about how someone out there is killing santhidyn. It *wanted* us to find it so that the news could spread."

"Let's hook the corpse," Rysn repeated, "and carry it to shore."

"No," several voices said from the crowd—but she couldn't see who. "That's bad luck!"

"If it's bad luck," Rysn said, her voice louder, "then we've already invited it by letting our hull touch the corpse. I say the best thing to do now is care for the body. We will burn the body, and leave the shell on a nearby island. We will purchase some floats at a port on our way home, and then tow it to Thaylen City. That's what the santhid would want: for us to keep the shell as a mark of the respect it showed us."

The crew fell silent. Rysn had taken part in her

fair share of tense negotiations, but this one made her hold her breath, her heart thundering. Like she was trying to contain a storm inside her.

"I think," the captain said eventually, "that I *do* see a good omen in this. I've always wanted to meet a santhid in the wild. I have burned prayers that one would someday come to me. This creature's soul must have known that."

"Yeah," another sailor said. "Notice how it doesn't stink? It should smell, rotting like that. I don't see a single rotspren. Good omen, that. It *wants* us to come near."

"Grab the hooks," the captain said. "If its spirit *is* restless, I certainly wouldn't want it thinking we ignored its last wishes!"

The sailors, blessedly, responded to her order. Rysn had given them an escape from their ill luck, and the captain had certified it. That was enough. Some went for the boarding hooks, which had ropes attached for use in holding the *Wandersail* to enemy ships. Others returned to their posts, to help keep the ship from drifting too far from the corpse.

The captain remained standing beside Rysn's chair. Tall, proud, in control. Rysn had learned to hold herself in a similar way, but she couldn't help being jealous of the ability to simply stand there. Exuding control and confidence was so much easier

when you weren't several feet shorter than everyone.

"Thank you," Rysn said to her.

"We have a charge from the queen to see this mission to its end," the captain said. "I'd turn around
now if I worried about losing my ship, but I won't do
so on a whim."

"Do you truly believe what I said about this being
a good omen?"

"I believe that passionate people make their own
luck," the captain said. Which wasn't exactly an
answer—the Passions, as a religion, believed that
wanting something changed fate to bring it to you.
Among many Thaylens, superstition and confidence
interwove like threads in a rope.

"Thank you, either way," Rysn said.

"For now, I trust your confidence to move forward, Rebsk," Captain Drlwan said as sailors returned with hooks. "Take care. This crew is precious
to me. I will not waste their lives if this mission turns
ugly." *If it turns out these omens are accurate,* she left
unsaid.

Rysn nodded and sat back, troubled, watching
the sailors cast the lines to hook the santhid body.
If they couldn't get a purchase, someone would
have to climb down and—

Sailors screamed, backing away, dropping the

ropes as if they'd suddenly burst aflame. Rysn started, then pulled herself up on the railing to look down. Was the santhid *alive*? It was moving. More undulating, quivering . . .

Disintegrating.

Before her eyes, the santhid broke apart into hundreds of scuttling pieces. Cremlings—crustaceans the length of a person's thumb—swarmed in the water. Rysn struggled to grasp what she was seeing. Had the hooks disturbed creatures that had been eating the dead santhid? But there were so *many*, and the entire beast was breaking apart. Including the shell.

Storms. It was as if . . . as if the body had been *made up* of cremlings. Or sealings, as the ones in the ocean were sometimes called. The water churned and frothed, and in moments nothing was left of the santhid. Even the eyeball she'd felt watching her earlier had broken into multiple pieces, exposing legs and shells on the underside, before swimming away into the deep.

9

Later that night, Rysn sat in a little cove, watching the bonfire send smoke toward the Halls far above. The chill air smelled alternately of the ocean and of smoke, depending on the whims of the wind.

She pulled her shawl closer. She often felt colder than others seemed to, though tonight she didn't call for Nikli to take her closer to the fire. She needed some solitude. And so she remained in her chair, some twenty or thirty feet apart from the others.

She listened as Lopen told stories to the sailors. Fortunately, his efforts to raise their spirits seemed to be working. After consulting with the captain, Rysn had ordered a shore landing to burn prayers in honor of the santhid. They'd broken out a few kegs of a special Thaylen ale, and Cord was cooking a stew. Cumulatively, their efforts seemed to mollify the crew.

The undercurrent of the evening, however, was still confusion. Everyone seemed as baffled as Rysn was. What kind of omen was *this*? A corpse appeared, then vanished? Had it been a corpse at all?

Nikli sat nearby. Chiri-Chiri slumbered on the ground next to Rysn. The larkin seemed to be getting worse. Sleeping more and more. Eating less and less. Rysn's heart trembled every time she thought about it.

Her spanreed finally began blinking. She snatched it up and oriented the board and pen, then let it start writing.

I have answers for you, the pen wrote. Vstim was dictating to his niece Chanrm, from the look of the handwriting. *The Alethi have been keeping a secret from you, and from me as well, though Queen Fen did know about it. While everything Queen Navani told you about the mission is true, there is another, more vital reason she commissioned this expedition. There was once an Oathgate on Akinah.*

Rysn read the words again, and let the implications sink in. An Oathgate. She hadn't tracked their locations. She probably should have.

Why did Aimia have one? she asked. *Wasn't it barren, all the way before the Recreance?*

No, Vstim wrote via his niece. *The scouring happened after that, though both were so long ago that we don't know many details. Apparently though, the capital had an Oathgate, like Thaylen City and Azimir. Queen Navani's team on your ship is supposed to investigate what happened to it.*

And open it? Rysn wrote back.

I gather they aren't certain they want it opened. Securing Aimia—particularly Akinah—would require a large military force. Right now, the queen merely wants information. Is the Oathgate there? Does it seem like the enemy has been investigating it? Is the island habitable?

So Nikli was right, the Radiants *had* been keeping things from her. At least their secret was a fairly innocent one. *What of the other thing I asked you about, Babsk?* Rysn wrote to Vstim.

On this matter, I've been less successful, he dictated. *None of the scholars I talked to have any idea what to make of your story of the disintegrating santhid. Though it does smell a little like some of the old stories about Aimians.*

That they could take off their arms and legs? Rysn wrote. *I met one of them on that expedition where I had my accident. That creature seemed very different from what we experienced.*

True, Vstim dictated. *But I spoke with Queen Jasnah Kholin about what you wrote to me, and she found it exceptionally curious. She says there were once two kinds of Aimians. One was the variety you saw. There are a few of them moving among the people of Roshar.*

As for the other . . . she read an old story to me about creatures that were living heaps of cremlings. They would grow in the attics of buildings, then devour the occupants. She says she once considered these stories fancies, no more real than things like the gloomdancer or sea hags from Thaylen mythology. However, she notes that recently she's begun hearing more reports of similar things—and from credible sources. She urges caution.

I'd appreciate any further information she can find, Rysn wrote. *If this were the only oddity we'd encountered, I wouldn't be so upset. But following the other items I mentioned, Babsk, it seems like a pattern. I think someone on the ship is deliberately trying to frighten my crew. And there might be an explanation that is more likely than these ancient stories.*

In what way? Vstim dictated. *How could some saboteur have created a santhid corpse like that?*

You remember what I encountered six months ago? Rysn wrote. *Right before the Battle of Thaylen Field? What if this was created by something like that?*

An enemy Lightweaver, Vstim dictated. *You think maybe someone made an illusion of a santhid corpse, then panicked as they realized you intended to tow it with you rather than sail away.*

Exactly, Rysn wrote. *And they made the illusion break into cremlings as a way of covering up what they'd done.*

But in that case, he dictated back, *wouldn't it mean an enemy Lightweaver is close? Potentially on the ship?*

Rysn didn't respond. That *was* what it would mean—though admittedly she didn't have a lot of experience with what Surgebinders could do or the range of their abilities.

I have a spanreed here to Queen Jasnah, Vstim dictated to her. *Just a moment. I am explaining your theory. I warned the others I would tell you what I had learned about the Oathgates. I made it clear that I did not appreciate one of my friends being sent on a dangerous mission without full knowledge.*

Rysn stared at the page. Friend? He was her master, her teacher. Honestly, her idol. Did he actually see her as a friend, now that she was grown? Something about that made her start to tear up.

All right, Vstim dictated, unaware of how that one word had affected her. *Queen Jasnah is agreeing with your theory. She wrote, "Of course, that is an astute observation. I should have seen that possibility. Our access to these powers is too new—we keep overlooking such things.*

"Compliment your shipowner for me, and warn her that an enemy Lightweaver is a very real possibility. And tell her that if there truly is one aboard, her mission is even more important, for it means the enemy is trying to prevent us from studying Akinah." From this woman, I think that is high praise, Rysn.

When the pen didn't write more, Rysn sent a reply. Well, I did almost get myself killed by one of those Lightweavers a few months ago. It's not cleverness on my part to consider them; more an instinct for self-preservation.

Yes, Vstim dictated. Rysn . . . perhaps sending you on this particular mission was unwise. The more I ponder it, the more I believe we should have sent a fleet instead of one ship.

Could we spare a fleet? Rysn wrote, though she knew the answer. Their navy had been dealt a serious blow when the parshmen—the Voidbringers—had turned. Most of the ships that remained were vital in escorting troop transports and preventing Thaylen City from being blockaded. So no, a fleet could not be spared for an expedition like this.

When no reply came, Rysn glanced at Chiri-Chiri sleeping on the stones beside her. Then she started writing again. Babsk, Rysn wrote, you trained me for difficult, remote work. You made a woman out of a *selfish child, and that woman is now prepared to use her expertise. I can do this.*

I do not doubt that you can, Vstim dictated back. *But I don't want anything else to happen to you in my service.*

She glanced at her numb legs, beneath the writing board. *I will be careful,* Rysn wrote. *And you have done a great deal for me already.*

Farewell, then, Vstim dictated. *I trust your judgment, but please understand that if you decide it is right to turn back, you should do so—regardless of what anyone says. You must lead this mission according to your wisdom.*

If only the crew had such faith in her. She said farewell to Vstim, then packed away her spanreed. After that, she looked up at the dark sky, searching for starspren and listening to the gentle crash of the waves. On her first few trips with her babsk, she'd been so self-absorbed—so frustrated at missing out on parties and negotiations with powerful houses— that she'd completely missed the beauty of this. Stars above, a sea breeze, and the soothing whispers of an ocean calling her to its embrace.

A soft sigh announced Nikli standing up nearby and stretching. He stepped over. "Brightness," he said, "it sounds like the food is ready. I'm curious to see if Cord's stew is better than mine. I'm going to get some for myself. Would you like a bowl as well?"

"In a while," Rysn said, looking out at the ocean. Little wavespren—like crawling four-legged creatures with smooth skin and large eyes—rode the foam up onto the beach, then quickly retreated with the water. "Your village is in . . . Alm, is it?"

"Yes, Brightness," he said. "Inland, up against the mountains."

"That's close to Aimia. Do your people have any legends or stories about the place?"

Nikli settled down on a large stone beside her chair. "We do. A lot of the survivors of the scouring settled nearby."

"Blue fingernails?" Rysn asked. "And vibrant blue eyes?"

"No, there were also ordinary people on Aimia," Nikli said. "Though they wear their beards in that odd way that's popular in Steen."

"Oh," she said. "What have they told you? About the scouring, about their homeland?"

"Brightness . . . the scouring was a long, *long* time ago. What we know are mostly myths, passed from generation to generation in stories and songs. I don't know if any of it would be useful to you."

"I'd like to hear them anyway," Rysn said. "If it's all right with you."

He watched the waves for a time. "It happened," he finally said, "because of the fall of the Radiants. Aimia had always been... different. The people who lived there. They were close with the Radiants, and maybe kept too many secrets. They assumed their secrets would protect them, but then their allies fell. And secrets can't hold swords.

"Suddenly they were alone in the world, and they possessed vast riches. It was just a matter of time. Perhaps some of the invaders were genuinely frightened of the oddities in Aimia. But most saw only the wealth. The fabrials, the creatures who could stop Shardplate, drain Stormlight." He hesitated, his eyes focusing on Chiri-Chiri. "I mean... that's what the legends say. I didn't give them a lot of credence until I met you."

"That's fascinating," Rysn said, getting out a fresh sheet of paper to record what he'd said. "Scholars around the world talk about Aimia in hushed tones. But I wonder, have they ever come and interviewed your people?"

"I'm sure they've talked to the human survivors," he said, looking down. "And there are immortals who lived on the island and now wander the world. I'm a poor source for information on this topic, Brightness."

"Nevertheless," she said. "What happened? How was the place scoured?"

"I don't know if my inadequate knowledge is of use to—"

"Please," Rysn said.

He continued watching the waves. A brave wavespren crawled all the way up the stone beach to their toes before turning and scuttling back into the water.

"Aimia shouldn't have existed, Brightness," Nikli said. "It . . . well, it should always have been like it is now. Barren. Too cold for much to grow. It isn't like Thaylenah, with favorable ocean currents nearby.

"But those old Aimians, they knew ways to make it lush, alive. There are . . . stories of fantastical devices that transformed Aimia from wasteland to paradise. I guess it was beautiful. I've imagined it that way, when hearing the stories. But . . ."

"But?" Rysn prompted.

"Well, the people who attacked Aimia quickly realized that destroying these devices would catastrophically undermine the place." He shrugged. "That's really all I know. Without these . . . fabrials, I guess they were? Without them, the island couldn't sustain a nation.

"Many were killed in the wars. Others fled. And the place has always been subject to unusual storms, so it became unlivable. It was looted, abandoned.

Those who survived came to live near us. And wept for their doomed paradise."

The melancholy in his voice made her look up from her writing. He glanced at her, then excused himself and went off to get something to eat. Rysn watched him go, tapping her pen against her paper. *Curious...*

Footsteps on the stones made her glance up to find a single figure—backlit by the bonfire—approaching. The Horneater woman, Cord, carrying a bowl of stew.

"Stew," she explained in Alethi, gesturing it toward Rysn. "I make. Try?"

Rysn accepted the bowl, feeling the warmth through the wood. It was good. Fish stew, with a unique blend of spices she'd come to associate with the Horneater woman's meals. The crew certainly enjoyed having her on board; her food was a huge improvement over the previous cook's offerings.

Rysn ate quietly as Cord settled down on the rocks beside her. "Captain?" Cord asked.

"I'm not the captain," Rysn said gently.

"Yes. I forget word," Cord said. "But...Brightness. Thing we saw. Corpse, becoming cremlings? I know of this thing."

"You do?"

"In Peaks," Cord said, "we have gods. And some are . . . I explain that this thing is . . . Ah, these words! Why do none speak ones that work?"

"The Horneater Peaks are in Jah Keved, right?" Rysn said, switching to Veden. "We can try this, if it's easier for you."

Cord's eyes went wide, and a single awespren—like a ring of expanding smoke—exploded behind her. "You speak *Veden*?"

"Of course," Rysn said, "it—" She cut herself off from saying it was very similar to Alethi, and easy to learn once you knew that language. Easy was a relative term, and these days Rysn was keenly aware that what was easy for one person could be a challenge for another. "It was part of my training as a trademaster. Alethi, Veden, Azish. Even some Iriali."

"Oh, *mala'lini'ka*," Cord said, taking her hand. "Someone who can speak a proper tongue. I wish I'd known this sooner. Listen. The creature we saw? The dead santhid? That is a *god*, not-captain Rysn. A *powerful* god."

"Interesting," Rysn said. "What kind of god?"

"My people know the gods well," Cord said, speaking quickly, eagerly. "There are gods that you call spren. There are gods that are like people. But some gods . . . some gods are neither. The one we met is of a group called the Gods Who Sleep Not."

"And they hide in attics?" Rysn said. "And devour the people who live in the homes?"

"*Tuli'iti'na,* foolish lowlander talk. Listen. They are a swarm of creatures, but they have *one* mind each. They have traveled our land, always as a creeping group of cremlings. They are not evil, but they are *extremely* secretive."

"I appreciate the information," Rysn said, thoughtful. "Can you tell me more of these gods who don't sleep?"

"Maybe," Cord said. "I know that lowlanders do not listen to our stories or think them true, but please understand. These gods guard treasures. Powerful, *terrible* treasures."

"That part sounds encouraging," Rysn said.

"Yes, but these gods are *so* dangerous, not-captain. They are associated with *apaliki'tokoa'a* who lead to treasure. . . . And the stories speak of trials. Tests."

"What do you think we should do? Turn back?"

"I . . . do not know," Cord said, wringing her hands. "I have no personal experience. My father might know more, if I were to write to him."

"Where is he?" Rysn said. "I will let you use my spanreeds, if they can reach him. I will listen to any information you find on these beings, no matter how insignificant it may seem at first."

"My father is at Urithiru," Cord said, gripping

her hand again. "Thank you. Yes, that would help. He—" She stopped and looked sharply at the sky.

"Cord?" Rysn asked.

"Spren," she said. "In the sky."

"I don't see any," Rysn said, frowning and glancing upward. "Did one of the stars move?"

"No, not starspren," Cord said. "*Apaliki'tokoa'a*. Lopen called them luckspren." She frowned. "They are swirling around in the sky, and keep darting toward the ocean, then returning. They dislike that we have delayed. They want us to continue our voyage."

"Wait," Rysn said. "I've seen luckspren flying with skyeels in the past. There aren't any in the sky right now."

"Oh!" Cord said. "You did not know? I see spren, even those that do not want to be seen. He is a gift, to my family, and others of my kin." She pointed. "There are twelve luckspren I count."

"Interesting," Rysn said. "Is that why the Radiants brought you?"

"Well," Cord said, "I think also Lopen wants to impress me? Maybe? Anyway, yes. I was uncertain at first, but was persuaded. The Radiants and Rushu wanted me to watch for spren that might have to do with Aimia. So I am here." She smiled. "You have *no idea* how nice this is to talk."

Well, that was one mystery cleared up. Cord's

presence on the trip finally made sense. But it was another secret Rysn couldn't understand why the Radiants had kept—save for the fact that they worked for the Alethi. It seemed that group kept secrets out of principle.

You work with the Thaylen guilds, Rysn reminded herself. *The Alethi aren't the only ones who weaponize information.*

"Cord," she said, a thought occurring to her. "Could you tell if someone was hiding behind an illusion? Perhaps if they were not human, but pretending to be, using Lightweaving?"

"I . . . do not think so," Cord said. She glanced at the sky again. "We must continue this voyage, Brightness not-captain. These spren are not high gods, but near to them. They urge us forward. But we must be cautious. . . ."

A call rose from the fire, and Huio waved for Cord to return—he was tending the stew in her absence—so she excused herself and hurried over. Rysn stirred at her bowl, taking bites but suddenly unable to enjoy the flavor.

In an odd way, she felt trapped. Between her own expectations and the very real worry that she was in over her head. Was she pressing forward stubbornly to prove herself, and endangering everyone? This seemed like the exact *wrong* time for Vstim to have turned to politics. His sailors needed him, and Rysn was a poor replacement.

She also worried so much about Chiri-Chiri. But was it right for her to endanger so many others to save one being? Both the Alethi queen and Cord encouraged her forward, but they weren't responsible for the lives of the *Wandersail*'s crew. Rysn was.

She needed to care for them. Even if they didn't trust her, or respect her. She needed to be the woman Vstim thought she was. Somehow.

Her ruminations were interrupted as Lopen, Huio, and Rushu left the fire and walked toward her. Sitting apart tonight had so far not quite accomplished her goal of solitude.

Rysn tucked her self-doubt away behind a tradeswoman's mask and nodded to them in welcome. They were speaking quietly in Alethi as they approached.

"He still feels bad," Lopen was saying. "But I worried about this. 'Huio,' I said to him, 'whenever you build a sandwich, you accidentally put the flatbread in the middle. How are you going to put back together a fabrial?'"

"Is true," Huio admitted. "Middle bread taste good."

"Your fingers get wet!" Lopen said.

"Wet fingers taste good," Huio said.

Rushu ignored them, instead kneeling beside Rysn's chair. It was her more comfortable one, padded and wider than the one with the wheels on the back legs. So it was broad and sturdy enough that Rushu could look all the way underneath.

"If you don't mind," the ardent said, then proceeded to start working on the bottom of the chair without waiting for a response.

Rysn blushed and tucked her skirts up tight against her legs. She did mind. People generally didn't understand how much Rysn saw her chairs as part of who she was. Fiddling with one was like touching her own person.

"In fact," Rysn said, "I would prefer if you asked first, Ardent Rushu."

"I did ask. . . ."

"Ask. Then wait for a reply."

Rushu hesitated, then pulled out from underneath the chair. "Ah. I apologize. Brightness Navani *did* warn me about how I act sometimes." She settled on her heels. "I have something I wish to try on your chair. With fabrials. May I proceed?"

"You may," Rysn said.

Rushu leaned forward and returned to work. Nikli approached, and shot Rysn a look that seemed to ask whether she needed help. Rysn shook her head. Not yet.

"Ardent Rushu?" Lopen asked. "I cannot help noticing that you have not given an explanation to me or Brightness Rysn about what it is you want to do."

"You say more than enough for both of us, Lopen," Rushu replied.

"Ha!" Huio said.

Lopen grinned, putting a hand to his head. "A fellow has to try all the words, sella, to see which ones make for good matches and which ones don't."

Rushu grunted her response from somewhere underneath Rysn.

"Words are like foods," Lopen said, settling down on the rocks nearby. "You've *gotta* taste them all. And foods change over time, you know. How they taste. What they mean."

"People change," Rushu said. "Your tastes change. Not the food."

"Nah, it's the food," Lopen said. "Because I'm still *me*, you see. I've always been me. That's the only thing I can really know—that I'm me. And so if the flavor of something changes, then the only thing I can say for *sure* is it tastes different, you know? So it changed."

"Huh," Rushu said. ". . . Lopen?"

"Yeah, sella?"

"Have you . . . had someone read you Pleadix's *Introspections*?"

"Nah," Lopen said. "Why?"

"Because that sounded almost like you were espousing—"

"Espousing?" he said. "I'm not married, sella. I suspect the ladies think there is too much Lopen—by at least one arm at this point, sure—for them to hold."

"Never mind," Rushu said. "Rysn, I *should* explain better. I apologize for that as well. You see, I discovered something alarming today."

"When we saw the santhid?" Rysn asked.

"Hmmm? Oh, no. I was napping during that. No, those two Windrunners were playing with my spanreeds this morning."

"Correction," Lopen said. "Huio was playing with them. I was being a responsible cousin and making fun of him for doing so."

"Right," Rushu said. "So Huio is solely to blame for this genius discovery, then."

"He exactly is . . ." Lopen paused. "Genius?"

"Genius?" Huio asked.

"He left a bit of foiled aluminum in the mechanism," Rushu said. "And it is interfering with the conjoined rubies in a *fascinating* way." She scooted back from Rysn's chair, then stood up and waved into the distance.

Rysn's chair shook.

"Oh!" Rushu said. "This is another part I should

have explained first, isn't it? Navani would be so upset with me. The rubies are connected to a chain and anchor—not the main anchor, don't panic! We don't want to send you into the stratosphere. Look over there, at that tree. See it? I had the sailors bring out one of the smaller anchors and tie it to ropes hung from branches."

In the distance, a sailor waved toward them. Rysn could make out a small anchor hanging from the tree nearby. Rushu pointed up into the air, and the sailors did something with the rope—

Rysn's chair lurched into the air about two feet. She cried out, grabbing the armrests. Chiri-Chiri finally woke up on the stone nearby, raising her head and chirping.

"It feels unsteady," Rysn said. "Should it wobble like this?"

"No," Rushu said, but she was grinning. "Huio, do you realize what you have done?"

"Make . . . wobbles?" he said. Then his eyes opened wide. "It wobbles! Wobbles—side-to-side!" He let out an exclamation in Herdazian that Rysn didn't understand, then grabbed Rushu's hand, barely able to contain his excitement.

Lopen folded his arms as he sat. "Will someone please explain how these wobbles are so entrancing?"

He gyrated his hips. "They do look fun, mind you. The Lopen approves of wobbling."

"If I may touch your chair, Brightness?" Rushu asked. "And nudge you to the side?"

"Go ahead," Rysn said.

Rushu gently pushed Rysn's chair—and it moved. She drifted a few feet to the side.

"This is supposed to be impossible!" Rysn said. "You said—"

"Yes," Rushu said. "Conjoined rubies are *supposed* to match each other's movement exactly. To move you two feet to the left, we should be required to move that anchor two feet to the right—which we aren't doing."

Rysn hovered there, trying to figure out the implications.

Huio said something in Herdazian and put a hand to his head, and two awespren in a row burst behind him. "It changes . . . all things."

"Well, maybe not *all* things," Rushu said. "But yes. This is important. Rysn, the aluminum is interfering with the mechanism, making the conjoinment uneven. The paired rubies still transfer vertical movement, but not lateral movement. So you will go up and down with the motion of the anchor, but then can move laterally in any direction you want."

"I need a pole," Rysn said, waving. "To see if I can do it on my own."

The Lopen found a branch for her from among some fallen limbs nearby. She used it to steady herself, then—biting her lip—she heaved against the rocks.

It worked. She soared a few feet through the air, as if she were gliding across water in her own personal gondola. She had to stop with the branch, because once she got going, there wasn't a lot to slow her except air resistance.

She tried to turn the chair around, but it resisted spinning. She was able to manage it only with some effort, then she poled back near her original spot.

"Hmmm," Rushu said. "You had to turn the anchor to spin. The mechanism must still have rotation conjoined; perhaps by experimenting with the aluminum we can fix that. At any rate, this is an amazing development."

"You're saying," the Lopen said, standing, "that by *breaking* your fabrial, Huio *fixed* it also?"

"More science happens through lucky accidents than you'd believe, Radiant Lopen," Rushu said. "It makes me wonder how many amazing innovations we've passed up because we were searching for something else, and didn't realize what we'd done.

"There's a chance I wouldn't have understood

the value in what Radiant Huio did if I hadn't been thinking specifically about Brightness Rysn's chair. As it was, when he brought me the broken spanreed, it was curiosity about her predicament that made me . . . Brightness? Are you well?"

They both looked to Rysn, who had been struggling to keep her composure as they chatted. She finally failed, and the tears started flowing. Chiri-Chiri chirped and leaped up, flapping her wings to help her get high enough to grab the chair with her mouth. Rysn scooped her up with one arm, holding to the branch with the other.

"I am well," she said with as much dignity as she could manage through the tears and the joyspren. "I just . . ." How could she explain? She'd tasted freedom, something forbidden her for two years. Everyone else pranced around without ever having to worry they were a burden to others. Never remaining in the same place—when they longed to move around—because they didn't want to be a bother. They didn't know what they had. But Rysn knew exactly what she'd lost.

"Hey," Lopen said, taking the arm of the chair to steady it. "Feels good, I bet. You deserve this, gancha."

"How can you know that?" Rysn said. "We've known each other for only a few weeks."

"I'm a good judge of character," Lopen said, with

a grin. "Besides. *Everyone* deserves this." He nodded to her, and a little windspren—in the shape of a one-armed youth—wandered through the air over to Lopen. Or . . . no, it wasn't a windspren. Something else.

A Radiant spren. It was the first time one had appeared to her, and this one bowed in a very official-seeming way. Then he broke into several copies, which all raised hands to wave at her.

"Forgive Rua," Lopen said. "He's a bit weird."

"I . . . Thank you, Rua," she said.

"I'm going to have to remove those gems on the chair for now, Brightness," Rushu said. "We'll need to use at least three for stability in the future, and I'll want to strengthen the housings. After that, we'll want to rig a way for you to order the anchor raised and lowered somewhere on the ship, so you can hover or not with a command."

"Yes, of course," Rysn said, but she clung to Chiri-Chiri as she was forced back to the mundane ground, the precious gemstones stolen away. She could bear it. Something better *was* coming. She saw independence, and it was glorious. Even if she could merely move about the deck of the ship on her own, pulling herself along the railing, it would be a huge improvement.

And the people who had helped her so much via

spanreed over the past few months? Gifting her the equipment they'd developed, urging her toward self-sufficiency? She would soon have a repayment for them. Oh, *storms* would she.

"Guess this will mean putting me out of a job," Nikli said, walking over.

Rysn felt a spike of worry for him. "For now this will only get me around the ship—if it ends up working. I suspect I'll have need of your strong arms for some time yet, Nikli."

However, he was smiling. "I would like nothing more than to be put out of this job, Rysn," he said softly. Then hesitated. "This is an important discovery for so many people. You should make certain to transfer it quickly via spanreed. So it is not lost, in case something happens to this expedition."

"Wise," Rysn said, glancing toward the dimming bonfire. The night was growing late. They'd soon need to get on the ship for the night. There was no storm today, and they'd be safer—in these foreign lands—out on the ocean than they would be trying to camp on the beach. "In fact, Ardent Rushu, you should probably inform others now. Don't sit upon this news."

Rysn gave the order to return to the *Wandersail*, and everyone started packing up. Rushu did as asked, while the Lopen explained to the sailors what had happened.

Nikli knelt beside her chair. "Brightness," he said. "It's not my place, I realize, to interfere in the doings of lighteyes. But . . ."

"Go ahead," Rysn said.

"Do you mind telling me what that Horneater said to you? Earlier?"

"We talked about spren, and about her gods. Why?"

"The other night," he whispered, "I overheard her saying something suspicious. She really wanted the expedition to continue. She's too eager. Something feels wrong, like . . . I don't know, Brightness. Like we're heading into some kind of trap."

"I think your suspicion is misplaced, Nikli," Rysn said.

"Maybe, maybe," he said, bobbing his head. "But earlier, did she warn you toward caution? Or did she encourage you forward?"

"She encouraged me forward *with* caution," Rysn said. "In that, she's no different from the Alethi queen, or Queen Navani, or even Queen Fen. All want us to succeed."

"Yet they keep secrets, lie to us," Nikli said. "I know I'm nobody important, Brightness. But if I were to come to you with proof of the Horneater's ill will toward us, would it help you see that something is wrong here?"

"I suppose it would," Rysn said, frowning. But why would Nikli be so worried? Though . . . Cord *had* used invisible spren only she could see as proof that Rysn should continue. And Navani *had* kept part of the truth from Rysn. About one thing, certainly. Perhaps about others?

But it made no sense. Cord was with the Radiants, and they trusted her. Why would Navani *ask* Rysn to go on this mission, then try to undermine it? Unless they were more divided than they seemed.

Or unless . . .

Her suspicion was piqued. "Thank you, Nikli," she said. "You were wise to bring this to me."

"I worry they're playing us for fools, Brightness," he whispered. "I don't like being manipulated to do Radiant work. Perhaps we should turn back?"

"Get me your proof first," Rysn said. "And for now, don't tell anyone what you've told me."

10

Rysn pulled herself along the port rail, and her chair—hovering in place a foot and a half off the deck—glided smoothly in response. She made it to the prow, then unlocked the mechanism that Rushu and Huio had installed on her seat. It was based on a spinning serving dish, and let the top of her seat rotate, while the bottom portion—with the gemstones—stayed in place.

Rysn spun around so she faced the other direction, then pulled herself back toward where she'd started. Because there was no real resistance once she began, it wasn't difficult work. But she did hold tightly to the rail, as she couldn't help imagining some situation where the ship turned and she somehow—despite the wall in the way—ended up hovering out over the ocean.

She soon reached where Nikli sat, the vibrant white tattoos that covered his face gleaming as he smiled. "That joy on your face, Brightness," he said, his voice lightly accented. "I don't know that I've ever seen it on a person before."

She grinned and turned her seat again, but this time locked it with her back to the rolling ocean so she could observe the working sailors. As the ship rocked on the waves, her chair threatened to slide to the side, and she had to reach out to Nikli to steady herself.

The mechanism needed some refinement—some way to attach her seat to the rail when she stopped. Still, she could barely contain her enthusiasm. Rushu had rigged a weight to the mast, connected via conjoined rubies, so Rysn could raise herself up to the height of the quarterdeck if she wanted. She couldn't lower her chair back down, unfortunately, without help to lift the counterweight—but for now she enjoyed more individual mobility than she'd ever had since her accident.

It felt wonderful. So good, in fact, that she turned and began pulling herself in the other direction again. And as she did so, she noticed the sailors watching her. Was it because of the oddity of her floating chair? Or because she risked interrupting their workflow, moving among them as she did? Though one of them nodded as she passed. And then another raised his fist toward her.

They're . . . rooting me on, she realized. In that moment she finally felt a kinship with the crew. A bond of understanding. What kind of person sought work on a sailing vessel? The type who longed for freedom—who wasn't content to sit where they were told, but instead wanted to see something new. A person who wanted to chase the horizon.

Perhaps she was imagining too much, but whatever their reasons, another raised a fist as he passed. The gesture seemed to propel her as she crossed the deck. As she swiveled and made her way back yet again, she noticed Cord stepping out onto the main deck.

It was time. Rysn nodded to Nikli, and he slipped off belowdecks. Rysn was about to have her suspicions confirmed; she tried not to think about how much it would hurt.

Cord took up a position near the prow. Ignoring her arms—which were beginning to ache from the difficulty of stopping and starting—Rysn turned and pulled herself that direction, eventually coming to a hovering rest beside the Horneater woman.

Rysn's chair put her a little higher than she was accustomed to sitting. If this worked, would she someday be able to hover in conversations at eye level with everyone else, even when they were all standing? A way to avoid feeling like a child among adults?

Cord was staring to the northwest. Over the last few days, they'd come within sight of Aimia—a large, windswept island roughly the size of Thaylenah. Rysn had received some additional information from Vstim—everything they knew about the scouring so many centuries ago—and it confirmed what Nikli had told her. The cold temperature of the surrounding waters and the general exposure to storms left Aimia barren. It was basically uninhabited to this day.

The smaller island they now thought was Akinah lay farther up along the coast, though it was unnamed on maps. Until recently, most scholars had assumed it to be one of the many islands clustered around Aimia that were now barren, nothing but crem and dust. And frequent localized storms in this region—along with treacherous rock formations just under the water's surface—historically made this region unpopular for sailors to explore.

Rysn could make out clouds on the horizon, their first indication that the ship was nearing its destination—the site of the strange weather pattern that they believed hid Akinah. Cord stared out at those clouds, holding to the rail, her long red hair streaming behind her in the wind.

"This next part might be dangerous, Cord," Rysn noted in Veden. "The *Wandersail* is a sturdy ship, among the best in the fleet, but no vessel is ever safe on rough seas."

"I understand," Cord said softly.

"We could go to port," Rysn noted. "There's a small watchpost on Aimia proper where our queen keeps a few men to survey the nearby seas for Voidbringer patrols. We could stop there to send spanreed messages and drop you off."

"Why . . . me?" Cord asked. "Why ask me?"

"Because our conversation earlier gave me the feeling you were forced on this trip," Rysn said. "And I want to make certain you are comfortable proceeding."

"I wasn't forced," she said. "I *was* hesitant, so your concern is appreciated. I want to go forward though."

Rysn held herself steady, hands on the rail, watching the shifting ocean. And those ominous clouds. "The Radiants I understand. They've been ordered to do this, like my sailors. Rushu is interested in the scholarly side, and I'm here for Chiri-Chiri. But you're not Radiant, Cord. You're not a soldier or a scholar. You're not even Alethi. So why join such a dangerous excursion?"

"They needed someone who could see spren," she replied, glancing up at the sky. "Fifteen today . . ."

"I understand why you were sent," Rysn said. "But not why you came. Does that make sense? Why did you *want* to join us, Cord?"

"I suppose he is a good question," Cord said, leaning on the railing. "You are a merchant. Always looking for what motivates people, right? Well, when I lived in the Peaks, I liked my home. My world. I never wanted to leave. But then I did, to join my father. And you know what I found?"

"A world?"

"A frightening world," Cord said, narrowing her eyes. "He is a strange place. And I realized that I liked him."

"Being afraid?"

"No. Being able to prove that I could survive frightening things." She smiled. "But as to why I came here? This trip? Treasure."

"Treasure?" Rysn said, glancing over her shoulder. Nikli hadn't returned yet. "That's it?"

"We have stories of this place, Akinah," Cord said. "Great treasure. I wanted some of him."

It seemed such a mundane answer, but Rysn supposed she shouldn't have been surprised. Wealth *was* the grand motivator that was common to all of humankind. It was part of why she'd become a trader, subjecting herself to apprenticeship.

But it felt . . . wrong to hear the words coming from this tall Horneater woman. She seemed so contemplative, so solitary. Was that really all there was to her? A desire for money?

"Well," Rysn said, "if we do find treasure, then we will all be wealthy."

Cord nodded curtly. She stood almost like a ship's figurehead. Rysn glanced over her shoulder again, and at last saw Nikli slipping up the steps. He caught her gaze and gestured urgently.

Rysn excused herself, then spun her chair and pulled her way over to the man. He leaned in, then took something from his pocket. A small pouch.

"What is it?" Rysn asked softly.

"Blackbane," he whispered. "A virulent poison, prepared in its strength. I found it hidden among the Horneater woman's things. Brightness . . . I think this is likely what was used to kill the ship's pet. The group from Urithiru didn't arrive on the ship until after the pet was dead, but they *were* in town the night before."

"How can you be certain this killed Screech?" Rysn asked.

"I've heard of this poison before," Nikli said. "It

is said to make a person's skin darken when it kills them, and I heard that poor Screech's skin was off-color when they found her. Brightness, it's clear now. The Radiants are lying to us. Why would they work so hard to undermine the trip?"

"Why indeed," Rysn whispered. She unfolded a small red handkerchief from her pocket and waved it. Kstled had been waiting for this; he rushed down the steps from the quarterdeck, hand on his sword, joined by two of his best soldiers. Lopen and Huio, who had been hovering near the ship instead of scouting outward as usual, dropped to the deck as well.

"Rebsk?" Kstled asked her. "Is it time?"

"Yes," Rysn said. "Take him."

Nikli didn't have time to so much as cry out. Kstled had him against the deck in seconds, a sturdy rope binding his wrists. It drew attention from the sailors, but the two armsmen waved them back to their work—and they went, knowing they'd get an explanation eventually. News didn't remain secret long in such close confines.

"What?" Nikli sputtered. "Brightness? What are you doing? I revealed the traitor to you!"

"Yes, you did," Rysn said. She'd had days to prepare for this event, ever since she'd become certain Nikli was the one creating the "omens." It hurt anyway. Damnation. He seemed so *genuine*.

Kstled finished binding Nikli and pulled him over and up to his knees. Nikli looked at her, and his next objections died on his lips. He seemed to know she wouldn't believe them.

"Of all the people I spoke to, Nikli," she said, "only you constantly tried to get me to turn back. And once you realized I wasn't accepting the omens, you saw me searching for the culprit. So you manufactured one for me."

He didn't respond, bowing his head.

"When I had Kstled thoroughly search Cord's room yesterday, we found no sign of this bag of poison in her things," Rysn said. "Yet you magically found one. Along with claiming expert knowledge on how it was used to kill the ship's pet."

"I see," Nikli finally said, "that you learned all of Vstim's lessons, Brightness."

"Being betrayed by someone you trust is painful beyond explanation," Rysn whispered. "But that is *never* a reason to pretend it can't happen."

Nikli sagged further.

"Why, Nikli?" Rysn asked.

"I . . . have failed. I will say nothing more, Rysn, but to beg you—with all sincerity—to turn back."

"I can make him talk, Brightness," Kstled said.

"I assure you, good man-at-arms," Nikli said— his accent having completely vanished. "There is *nothing* you can do to me that will get you the answers you desire."

Radiant the Lopen stepped closer. She hadn't shared her entire plan with him, but had given him enough. She knew firsthand the danger of the Fused Lightweavers. If Nikli was one of those, she wanted a Radiant ready to face him.

At her request, the Lopen scooped Chiri-Chiri from her cloth nest on the quarterdeck, then brought her to Rysn. Kstled stood and pulled Nikli to his feet, bound. Rysn held Chiri-Chiri up toward him, and the larkin lethargically chirped.

"Anything?" she asked the larkin.

Chiri-Chiri clicked, but didn't otherwise respond. Rysn pulled her back and offered her a sphere, which thankfully she consumed.

"I don't think he's hiding Stormlight or Voidlight," Rysn said to the soldiers. "But I can't be certain." She scratched Chiri-Chiri where her carapace met skin. If Nikli was secretly an enemy servant, Chiri-Chiri would have drained his Light away.

At her command, Kstled sent two armsmen to search through Nikli's things. She watched closely, but the captive man showed no sign of Voidbringer powers; he merely drooped in his bonds.

"Tell me, Nikli," Rysn said. "When we search *your* things, what will we find? Proof that you're the one who poisoned the ship's pet and put the worms in our grain?"

Nikli refused to meet her eyes.

"You want me to turn back," Rysn said. "Why? And how did you do that trick with the santhid?"

When Nikli didn't respond, she looked to the Lopen.

"There's no way to tell if he's a Fused, gancha," he explained. "At least, no way *I* can tell. Queen Jasnah, sure, she could do it. But to Rua and me, he looks like a regular person. Even cutting him won't work. A regular singer, they would bleed blood the wrong color. But a Lightweaver? Well, he could change that."

"Could we have Cord inspect him?" Rysn asked. "And see if she spots any strange spren?"

"Worth a try," the Lopen said, and went to fetch her. Rysn didn't expect much, unfortunately. Cord had been around this man for the entire trip. If there had been something to spot, surely she would have noticed it already.

Indeed, after a quick inspection, Cord just shrugged. "I don't see anything unusual," she said in Veden. "I'm sorry."

"We've taken his assistant captive, Brightness," Kstled said softly. "Just in case."

"Plamry knew nothing of this," Nikli muttered.

"What do we do with him?" Kstled said.

Normally, she'd have thrown him in the brig. Plamry too, as she wasn't certain she could trust the man. But her ship was approaching a mysterious storm. Traversing that, then exploring the island beyond, would consume her crew's attention. Did she really want a possible Voidbringer sitting in her hold?

Unfortunately, if he *was* a Voidbringer, executing him would do no good—he would simply claim a new body at the next Everstorm. And if he wasn't one, she keenly wanted to interrogate him once the mission was finished.

"Cord," she said. "A moment, please." Rysn pulled herself a little way to the side, and Cord joined her. "If he were a servant of one of those . . . gods you told me about," Rysn whispered in Veden, "the ones that guard treasures? Would there be a way to know?"

"I have no idea," Cord said softly. "The Gods Who Sleep Not are powerful. Terrible. Cannot die. Cannot be captured. Eternal, without body, capable of controlling cremling and insect."

Delightful.

"Radiant the Lopen," Rysn called, "would you and Huio fly our captives to the main island of Aimia? Bring some manacles and lock them to whatever convenient feature you find. Give them some food and water. We'll leave them, and recover them after exploring Akinah."

"Sure thing, gancha," the Lopen said.

It wasn't a perfect solution; she fully expected Nikli to have found a way to escape by the time they returned for him. But at least she'd have him off her ship. Voidbringer, god, or simple traitor, this seemed the best way to protect her crew. She'd send word of his location to the Thaylen watchpost. Plamry, at least, might be innocent. She didn't want him left alone if something happened to the *Wandersail*.

One of her sailors arrived with manacles, and Rysn watched—discomforted—as Nikli and Plamry were flown off. Storms, did she need to suspect every member of her crew of being an enemy Lightweaver?

The only thing she could do would be to have the captain and Kstled interview every crewmember, to search for anyone who seemed off. Kstled went to join Captain Drlwan on the quarterdeck—she'd been informed ahead of time, of course. She would make an announcement to the crew.

Eventually, the sailors sent to rummage through Nikli's things returned with another bag of poison and, curiously, an annotated recipe book written in Azish.

Rysn looked through this, finding notes that said things like, "Humans prefer salt in abundance" or "cook longer than you think will be required, as they often eat their meals mushy." And, most alarmingly, "This will cover the taste" in reference to a spicy dish.

The implications haunted her. If his attempts to get them to turn back hadn't been successful, would Nikli have poisoned the crew? It made a terrible kind of sense—they'd have needed another cook if Cord was imprisoned, and Nikli had bragged to her about his cooking ability. She could see a world where he was put in charge of the ship's galley, and the rest of them unwittingly ate his deadly meal.

It was time to put some extra precautions in place. A few rats tasting each meal before it was served to the crew, perhaps?

Who are you really? she wondered at the distant figure. *And why are you so intent on keeping us away from this island?*

11

The Lopen gained new respect for the Thaylen sailors as the ship breached the storm around Akinah.

He'd spent the last few weeks sitting with them at meals, climbing with them on the rigging, scrubbing the deck alongside them, or swapping stories as they swung in their hammocks at night. He'd even picked up a little Thaylen. He was living on a sailing ship, so he figured—sure—the best way to pass the time was to follow Huio's example and try to become a sailor.

Lopen had heard them talk about the terrifying experience of facing down winds and rain while on the sea. You didn't sail a storm, they'd explained. You hung on, tried to steer, and hoped to survive until the end. He'd felt the frightened tone in their voices, but

Damnation, he felt something ten times worse as the *Wandersail* headed into the strange storm.

He'd flown about in storms, sure. He was a Windrunner. But this was different. Something primal inside him cringed as the wind made the water churn and froth. Something that trembled as the darkening sky painted the ocean with new ominous shadows. Something deep in his heart that said, "Hey, Lopen. This was a baaaaad idea, mancha."

Rua, naturally, took it with a grin on his face, having adopted the shape of a skyeel with human features. He swam through the air around Lopen's head as the ship began to sway like a child's toy in the bath.

"Lopen!" Turlm called, rushing past with a rope. "You may want to get belowdecks. It's about to get wet up here!"

"I won't melt, hregos!" Lopen called back.

Turlm laughed and continued on. Good man, Turlm was. Had six daughters—*six*—back home in Thaylen City. Ate with his mouth open, but always shared his booze.

At his warning, Lopen took a solid hold on the railing. It was strange to see the ship stripped of most of its sails, like a skeleton without the flesh. But this ship, sure, was special. Fabrial pumps would supposedly keep it bailed, no matter how much water washed onto the deck. And there were stabilizers that used attractor fabrials. Those would shift weights around in the hull—crazy, that stuff was built *inside* the hull—and keep the ship from capsizing.

At the captain's orders, the oars came out. They used those for fine maneuvering when trying to ram enemy ships, but here they could reposition the ship to take big waves the right way. When caught in bad weather, ships would try to "run" the storm. That meant going with the wind, only in a specific way that sounded extremely technical to Lopen. He'd nodded anyway, since the words had been quite interesting, particularly coming from the lips of mostly drunk men.

They couldn't simply run the storm here though. They had to breach it, reach its core. So they'd follow the storm in a loop around Akinah, slowly edging inward, ever inching toward the center. And they had to keep ahead of the waves, which meant sometimes colliding with other ones in front. They'd need to "head" those waves: keep the ship going straight at them, breaking them across the bow. The oars would help keep them positioned for that.

It felt downright heroic to meet these winds with only one small stormsail maintained by a few valiant sailors. The rest were below, either at the oars or maintaining the fabrials. Lopen didn't see how the sail wouldn't just blow them all over the place, but they all said it would work. They'd also tied bags of oil over the side of the ship too, with punctures to leak—which they said would keep the water from spraying so much on the deck.

The captain stood firm and shouted her orders into the wind, sending them straight into the gullet of the beast. And by the Halls themselves, if the sailors didn't take it with determination and grit.

The wind picked up further, blowing sprays of water across Lopen's face. Huio hadn't wanted to come up above, had said Lopen was crazy for insisting on being on deck. And yes, cold water began to seep through his unders to prickle his skin. But storms, it was an incredible view. The lightning made the water seem to spark, transparent, and huge froths of it surged into the air. A storm on land was a sight to behold, sure, but a storm on the waters . . . this was *majestic*. Also horrifying.

"This is amazing!" Lopen said, pulling himself along the railing so he was closer to Vlxim, the day's helmsman. Three other men stood at the ready to help Vlxim wrestle the wheel to control the rudder. That was common on ordinary ships, but this one had some kind of mechanism to help the helmsman, and so it might not be needed.

"You haven't seen anything!" Vlxim shouted. He was bald like Huio, which made his eyebrows look extra amusing to Lopen—particularly wet as they were. But he played a mean mouth harp. "We've trained to sail into highstorms on this ship if we have to! I've actually *been* through one! Waves as high as mountains, Lopen!"

"Ha!" Lopen said. "*You* haven't seen anything. I was once in a place where Everstorm and highstorm met, and in *that*, the rock flowed like water and—sure—entire chunks broke like waves against one another. I had to run up one side, then slide down the other. Ruined my storming trousers!"

"Enough!" the captain yelled over the wind. "I don't have time for you two to compare sizes. Vlxim, one point to port!"

The captain eyed Lopen, and he gave her a salute—because they were on her ship, and here she outranked even the people who outranked her. But he got the feeling that the captain was the kind of person who had been born an officer, coming right on out of her mom with a hat on and everything. People like that didn't understand; bragging wasn't about making yourself look good, but about convincing the other guy you weren't afraid, which was *completely* different.

A wave surged over the deck, and Lopen lost

his footing, but clung onto the ship's aft rail and grinned—sopping wet—at Vlxim when he glanced over. Lopen righted himself with effort, and thought about Vlxim's words. How could waves get *bigger* than these? They sailed up the side of one that Lopen could have *sworn* was too steep to ride. Then they went crashing through the top, like Punio through a crowd on his way to the privy after a night of drinking.

Lopen whooped as they teetered, then came rushing down the wave's other side. Rua swirled about him as a ribbon of light, excited, dancing with the wavespren—who went splashing high into the air as different waves met. This was the best time they'd had in ages.

Then Turlm—the fellow who had passed Lopen with the rope earlier—got caught in an unexpected wave and washed clean off the deck. Into the drink, the dark abyss, to be claimed by the seas and strangled with water.

Well, couldn't have that.

Lopen burst alight and leaped over the rail, Lashing himself toward the water. He hit with his own crash, pulling in so much Stormlight he glowed brightly in the dark water—revealing a struggling figure being swept away in the currents. Well, Lopen had spent a few days practicing this while out on the ocean, doing scouting runs. Lashings worked fine underwater. And hey, who needed to breathe when you had Stormlight?

He Lashed himself toward the dark figure—Rua guiding the way—and blasted through the ocean like some kind of underwater creature built to move through it easily and swiftly. Or, well, like a fish. They called those fish, didn't they?

Lopen grabbed hold of the struggling form by his clothing, then Lashed both of them upward. Rua pointed the way—it could be surprisingly difficult to tell directions in the darkness underwater. Lopen exploded from the ocean a moment later, carrying a sputtering Turlm.

Rua darted ahead, leading him toward the ship— which was good, because in the dark tempest, details were about as easy for Lopen to make out as his own backside. Lopen hauled Turlm over the rail and hit the deck with a thump, then Lashed the man in place so he wouldn't go sliding off again.

"Storms!" Fimkn said, stumbling over to help the other sailor. Fimkn had a medic background, and he and Lopen had bonded over the fact that both had been told too many storming times to boil bandages. "How did you . . . Lopen, you saved him!"

"It's kind of our thing," Lopen said.

Turlm sputtered, then started laughing uncontrollably. Joyspren like little blue leaves spun around him, then swirled into the air. He gripped Lopen's hand in thanks. The old one. His Bridge Four hand, not his Knight Radiant hand. Fimkn sent Turlm belowdecks—a replacement had already come up to take his post—so Lopen un-Lashed him. Storms, that replacement had shown up quickly. They were *expecting* to lose people. Or at least they were prepared for it.

Well, not on Lopen's watch. You didn't let your friends drown in nameless oceans during a frigid storm. That was, sure, basic friendship rules right there.

He marched back up onto the quarterdeck. The captain and the others here had ropes to hold them in place, but those had to be short, and didn't generally work for the other sailors, who needed a lot of freedom of movement. A long rope on a man who got swept overboard in this kind of storm broke necks and smashed sailors into the hull. The chances were better, though still slim, without ropes.

Lopen figured he should be extra careful with the captain anyway. With her permission, he stuck one of her feet to the deck, so she could move a little—but had one really steady foot to rely upon.

"You could have done that all along?" the captain asked. "I saw you struggling to keep upright earlier! You were sliding about with the waves. Why didn't you stick yourself down?"

"Didn't seem sporting!" Lopen called over the increasingly loud sounds of the storm. "You keep us going straight, Captain. I'll watch the crew!"

She nodded, and turned to her task. Running with the winds, but—best they could—on their own terms. He had to trust she was keeping the ship on its spiral heading, moving steadily inward. Because he couldn't make any sense of this. The sea seemed to be Damnation itself, incarnate as furious waves.

Lopen kept an eye on the sailors, but he had Rua watching something else. Eventually—after splashing through wave after wave—the little honorspren came zipping up to Lopen in the shape of a skyeel with an extremely long tail.

"What is it, naco?" Lopen asked.

Rua pointed at the water nearby, and Lopen saw a shape in the depths—or at least a dark shadow. Size was difficult to judge because he didn't know how deep the thing was, but Rua was insistent. It was one of them. The things that had feasted on Stormlight, draining the Windrunners who had tried to investigate the storm before.

"It's swimming?" Lopen asked, wiping rainwater

from his eyes. "How can you be certain that's one of them, naco?"

Rua simply was. And Lopen trusted him. He figured, sure, Rua would know about this sort of thing, same as Lopen knew about one-armed Herdazian jokes.

Leyten and the others hadn't been able to report much about the things. They *thought* they were alive, not spren, but couldn't be certain. The things had needed to get close to them though, so it probably couldn't affect Lopen up here on the deck. Leyten said they'd hovered out in the clouds, indistinct, until he turned—then they'd come in from behind and drained him.

But were they the same type of creature as what Rysn kept as a pet? This one in the water seemed far larger. And more blobby somehow? Lopen would need to be careful when rescuing other members of the crew—if that thing drained him while he was in the drink, it would be catastrophic. He'd have to learn some dead Herdazian jokes to tell in the afterlife.

The sailing continued a long, terrible time. Lopen kept a vigilant watch through it all, and so was ready when Wvlan lost his footing. Lopen was on him before he was swept overboard, and pulled them both up against the rail and stuck them there, water cascading over them. He gave Wvlan a pat and a laugh, but when Lopen got to his knees to let the water stream off him, he noticed the dark shadow in the water right over the side of the ship. Keeping pace with them.

He wished he could get Cord out here to see if any strange spren were nearby. But he didn't dare bring her into this storm. It would be—

The ship crashed through one final wave, and the wind abruptly stopped. Amazed, Lopen stumbled to his feet, then wiped his eyes again. Nearby sailors relaxed, loosening their grips on the ropes they'd been using to do . . . well, some sailor things with the stormsail.

"We made it!" Klisn said. "Storms, it's like the centerbeat!" An awespren burst around him, and Lopen agreed with the sentiment. The rough waves and wind blew in a circular pattern right behind them. Dark clouds still blocked the sky, but the ship cut through choppy smaller waves, settling into a peaceful rest here—where even the waters seemed less dark, more sapphire than they had on the way in.

"Hey, Klisn?" Lopen said. "Would you go fetch Cord for me? I told her I'd get her as soon as it was safe, but I should go unstick your captain from the deck. I suspect she is liking it about as much as Punio did during the weeks I had a spren and he did not."

"Sure thing, Lopen," Klisn said, running off. He was a great fellow. Skilled partner at cards, plus he had an excellent sense of humor. And not only because he thought Lopen's jokes were funny. He also thought Huio's were terrible.

Lopen hastened up the stairs to the quarterdeck, then slowed as he stepped up beside the captain and helmsman. They were staring out across the ocean, toward something emerging from distant fog. An island.

It was surrounded by big stone spikes rising out of the ocean like a wall somehow built in the sea itself. But there was a huge gap where a dozen or more had either been removed or never placed. As the ship drifted farther, the waters stilled in an eerie way. The gap revealed a shallow island, small enough that Lopen could probably walk around the perimeter in an hour or so. Near the center, he spotted what he thought must be city walls, and maybe some structures near them.

"Well, hie me off to Damnation," the captain muttered. "It's actually real."

12

We're here, Chiri-Chiri," Rysn whispered as several of the sailors set her into her chair on the quarterdeck. "Look. I've brought you home."

Chiri-Chiri nestled into her arms and barely moved. Rysn held her close as the captain and her brother conversed quietly nearby. Storms . . . the island looked so . . . surreal, with that too-still ocean, the distant fog, that strange rock palisade in the waters around it. The island itself was low and flat, except for that part near the center. Were those walls or a natural plateau?

The crew had gathered on deck, mingled with anticipationspren, like red streamers waving in an unfelt wind. Rysn wasn't close enough to hear what they whispered to one another, and she almost tried to pull herself along the rail to get closer. Only a few days with her hovering chair, and already she relied on it.

Well, if this place turned out to be an enemy stronghold, they might have to leave quickly. She didn't want to risk the floating chair, so she'd ordered it stowed and had the gemstones in her pocket. Her quarterdeck seat would have to do.

So she sat quietly, trying not to feel overwhelmed. They were here, finally. Rysn had brought them here. How would Vstim have proceeded? She didn't know. She had learned his wisdom, but now she simply had to trust her own instincts.

That was more frightening to her than it had ever been before. "Captain," she said, calling toward Drlwan. "What do you think? What news from the eel's nest?"

The woman strode over. "I have three men with spyglasses searching for anything suspicious," the captain said. "No signs of life, though there are definitely structures farther in. Not much wind here, oddly, but we can use oars to maneuver. These waters look treacherous, so we'll want to go slowly. The depths around Aimia often have hidden hazards beneath the surface.

"Assuming all goes well, we could maneuver through that gap and get in close to the island." She hesitated. "Rebsk, the lookouts report what appear to be gemhearts on the beach. Just lying there, discarded among the shells of fallen beasts."

Curious. Rysn took a deep breath. "I authorize a slow approach. Warn me if anything new is spotted, and kindly have someone ask the Radiants and their party to come speak with me." She could see Lopen, Huio, and Rushu chatting softly with Cord down on the main deck.

The captain ordered some of the sailors to man the oars, and soon they were gliding carefully toward the ring of tall rocks that surrounded the island. They reminded her of the obelisks the Deshi nomads set up at their various waystops.

Eerily, the only sounds were those of the oars on the water—a stark counterpoint to the raging winds and waters they'd left behind. As they moved—checking depth on both sides of the ship every minute or two—the Radiants and their friends stepped up onto the quarterdeck.

"What do you see, Cord?" Rysn asked in Veden.

"Luckspren," she said, pointing overhead. "But they're not approaching the island. There are dozens upon dozens flying around out here. Lopen showed me a shadow of something under the water that he thinks might be what drained Stormlight from the other Radiants, but I saw no spren. The shadow vanished quickly, but I think he must be *toa*, not *liki*. Um, I think you say physical, and not . . . mind? Of the mind world?"

"Curious," Rysn replied, though she wasn't entirely certain she understood.

"Hey," Lopen said. "You speak . . . um . . . is that . . ."

"Veden," Rysn said in Alethi. "I do."

"I might be able to get the ship through that gap," the captain said, walking over. "How would you like to proceed, Rebsk?"

"Take us as close as you dare, Captain," Rysn said.

Drlwan skillfully guided them up to the gap and, after another check of depths, sailed the ship right through the opening. The captain brought them in close enough to the island that Rysn could make out bleached carapace on the shore—the remnants of ancient greatshells. Again she held up Chiri-Chiri, hoping to get some reaction. Talik had said they should come here. But what now?

Chiri-Chiri didn't seem interested in the place, though she did look up toward the sky and then stirred, chirping softly. Rysn placed Chiri-Chiri carefully in her lap, and the creature didn't move much, but did keep her attention on the sky. Could she sense those invisible spren, perhaps?

Kstled stepped up and handed Rysn a spyglass. Through it, she easily made out the carapace husks as well as large diamond gemhearts lying scattered around. Dun, showing no light, they lay as if they'd fallen right where the beasts had died. Something about that struck her as odd.

"Orders, Rebsk?" the captain asked her.

Orders. It was time to be in charge. She ignored her fluttering heart, her worry for Chiri-Chiri. "Radiant the Lopen and Ardent Rushu. I assume you two will want to be on with your secret mission?"

The two shared a glance, and were embarrassed enough to draw a few shamespren, like floating flower petals.

"Er, yes, Brightness," Rushu said. "We'll want to strike inward, toward those buildings."

"I suggest letting my men do a quick reconnaissance before you do so," Rysn said. "Kstled, take a large contingent of sailors and—leaving non-combatants on the ship for now—secure the beach. Report anything unusual."

He bowed to her, then went to gather the sailors. As the rowboats were lowered, Lopen and Huio climbed aboard. So did Rushu.

"Ardent Rushu?" Rysn called after her. "I suggest you wait until we're certain the beach is safe."

"A fine suggestion!" Rushu called back. "But don't worry about me, Brightness." And she settled herself on the bench of one of the boats.

Well, she wasn't technically under Rysn's authority.

So she could do as she wished. Cord wisely didn't insist on going—instead she knelt beside Rysn's chair, then turned her gaze from Chiri-Chiri up toward the sky.

Was there a connection between the luckspren and Chiri-Chiri? Skyeels were the only other creature her size that could fly, and they were often accompanied by luckspren.

Chiri-Chiri chirped again, an encouraging sign. Rysn gave her a sphere to eat, then glanced over her shoulder toward the storm. The fog obscured much of that, but in clearer patches she could see a sweeping barrier of wind and tempest. Like the stormwall of a highstorm, only blowing circularly.

"We should finish this as quickly as possible," Rysn said to Drlwan, who still stood nearby. "Once we're certain the shore is safe, have some of the sailors begin scouting around the perimeter of the island. We can collect any interesting artifacts and give the Radiants time to—"

Chiri-Chiri thrashed in her lap. Rysn looked down as the creature perked up for the first time in weeks, then stood, her wings fluttering. She was still staring at the sky.

"Cord?" Rysn said in Veden. "Is she seeing luckspren?"

"I think so," Cord said. "They've begun to fly lower."

Rysn squinted, and believed she could see them. Faint arrowhead figures shimmering in the air. Chiri-Chiri chirped louder. Rysn found her heart beating faster, her breaths quickening. She'd begun to worry that this had somehow all been in vain, that there would be nothing here to help Chiri-Chiri.

The larkin zipped into the air. Storms, it had been forever since she'd flown so energetically!

The luckspren began moving more quickly. Rysn lost sight of them, and Cord gasped. Chiri-Chiri immediately tucked and dove straight down *into the water.*

Rysn cried out, her excitement bleeding into panic. She twisted and leaned over the side, joined by Cord. Chiri-Chiri swiftly vanished into the shadows, moving beneath some rocks and out of sight.

"She followed the spren..." Cord whispered. "Something is happening. Something is odd...." She narrowed her eyes.

The captain stepped to the rail. "Did...you know it could swim?"

Rysn shook her head, feeling an alarming spike of loss. What if...what if Chiri-Chiri never came back? What if by bringing her here, Rysn had unwittingly offered her freedom—and she'd taken it? Well . . . Rysn tried to be positive. That *was* better than Chiri-Chiri being sick. And if the creature wanted freedom, Rysn wouldn't confine her.

At the same time, so much emotion was wrapped up in her experiences with the larkin. Rysn's slow recovery from her accident, her year of melancholy, her near death at the hands of Voidbringers. Chiri-Chiri had been with her for all that, and—in that brief first moment wondering if she was alone—Rysn found a startling fragility to her feelings. A desire to cling to something she loved and never, *never* let go.

Was that selfish? A trade or exchange couldn't be a good one unless both parties gained something from it. Yet not everything was about exchanges and trades. It was sometimes difficult for her to remember that.

"Rebsk?" the captain asked.

"I . . . will wait here to see if she returns, Captain," Rysn said, trying to remain steady. "Please, bring me word from the shore party as soon as they've inspected the beach."

13

Lopen stood dramatically at the prow of the small boat, one foot up, spear over his shoulder, Rua standing in exactly the same pose on his other shoulder. The sailors had unshipped their oars behind him, as the rowboat now moved along under its own power. Why make the sailors work when you had Lashings?

Besides, Lopen could see a shadow under the water, moving along with him. These waters were shallow now, but whatever it was stayed close to the bottom—and with the clouds in the sky, it was dark enough down there to prevent Lopen from making out what it was.

He was still convinced, however, that this shadow was the thing that could feed off Stormlight. But not a little one like Chiri-Chiri. This was bigger, and a different shape. Flatter? It was hard to tell. He'd hoped it would surface and try to steal the Stormlight he put into the rowboat.

It didn't. It seemed . . . timid. Frightened of him, unwilling to confront him directly. So Lopen tried to keep an eye on it, and had Rua do the same. It was hard, considering how exciting this next part was going to be.

Ahead, the water gave way to a rocky beach— which was overgrown with storming *gemhearts* like they were rockbuds. The chitinous remains of greatshells watched over them with hollow, cavernous eyes. Discarded armor of beasts long dead.

Huio's boat drifted up beside Lopen's, then slowed to match his lazy speed as they crossed the bay. Lopen's cousin crouched, holding his spear in a tense posture.

"Can you believe it, older-cousin?" Lopen said. "Stepping foot on a land no person has ever visited."

"There was a city here, Lopen," Huio said. "It was literally one of the capitals of the Epoch Kingdoms."

"Well, yeah," Lopen said. "But, sure, there's got to be a portion of it nobody ever stepped on, right?"

"I wouldn't bet on that," he said. "Considering how long the Epoch Kingdoms stood and the expected population numbers."

"Fine," Lopen said, pointing forward heroically,

with Rua copying him. "Onward we go, to step foot on a land no person has visited in centuries!"

"Except the crew of that other ship," Huio said. "Who probably landed on the island, since they weren't found on their ship. And others who presumably killed those people. We'll be the first, except for all those."

Lopen sighed and glanced at Rua, who rolled his head from one shoulder to another in annoyance, then made it fall off. "Cousin," Lopen said, "do you know why it is that people stick you to the wall so often?"

"To judge the relative strength of Radiants by oath level, measuring the duration of Lashings against the Stormlight expended."

"It's because you're no fun."

"Nah, I decided to let it be fun. You get an entirely new perspective on life when hanging from the wall." Huio grinned, then both of them turned sharply. The shadow under the ocean had changed direction, slipping away back toward deeper waters. Apparently it didn't want to rise up high enough to let them get a good look at it.

Lopen's Lashing ran out right as the boat ground against the stones and beached itself. As it jerked to a halt, he used the momentum to tip forward and step straight onto the shore. Now *that* was style. He glanced around to see if anyone had noticed. Too bad Cord was on the ship, waiting until the sailors had scouted the region.

Sailors jumped out of the other large rowboats, then had to wade through the water to pull them ashore. Rua watched that with sadness.

"You could go run through the water if you want, naco," Lopen said.

Rua glanced at him, still sitting on Lopen's shoulder in his small form, then cocked his head.

"Well, yes," Lopen said. He always knew what Rua meant. It was the way things were. "Just because I have style landing with elegant dignity and control doesn't mean those fellows *lack* style when running through the waves. They have sailor style, while I've got the Lopen style." He tapped Rua on the nose. "Don't let people tell you that style is limited, pretending it will run out like Stormlight. Style is the best resource in the world, because we can make as much of it as we want—and there's plenty, sure, for everybody."

He put his hands on his hips and studied the beach, then ran over to help Rushu get out of her boat, because ardent style—with all those pieces of paper—did *not* involve getting wet.

"Thank you, Radiant Lopen," she said as she tucked her notebook under her arm. A sailor who climbed out after her carried her spanreed and other equipment. "So, what do we make of this?"

"There's money," Lopen said, waving toward the diamond gemhearts with his spear, "lying on the storming ground."

"Yes, curious," Rushu said.

"Dead . . . place?" Huio said. "Place of dead?" He cursed softly in Herdazian, trying to find the right Alethi words.

"Oh!" Rushu said. "I'll bet this is a place where greatshells come to die. I've read of that sort of thing. I'll have to write to Brightness Shallan; she studies greatshell life cycles."

Kstled walked up, his back straight as the ship's mast, a barbed spear over his shoulder and a short-sword at his waist. "I suppose," he said, gesturing to the riches, "these are cursed, and I should forbid my men from indulging?"

"Don't be silly," Rushu said, writing something in her notebook. "We're here to loot the place, armsman Kstled. Have the men heave ho or whatever and get on with it. I want to sleep in a bed of boundless lucre tonight."

"Aren't you . . . an ardent?" Kstled asked. "And therefore forbidden personal possessions?"

"Doesn't mean a lady can't lie on a big heap of gemstones," Rushu said. "They talk about it in the stories. I've always wondered how uncomfortable it would be."

She looked up from her notebook, wide-eyed as she regarded them all. "What? I'm serious. Go! Gather it all up! We were sent to collect artifacts from this place, and those gemstones absolutely count. Though perhaps remind the sailors that they'll get their traditional percentage share from this salvage, so they'll all be rich when we return—assuming they don't try to hide anything or steal from the others."

"Assign me several of your best, Kstled," Lopen said. "Once Brightness Rysn approves, I'll take them and the ardent and scout inward. See what we find off the beach."

Well, see if they could locate the Oathgate. But he wasn't supposed to talk about that part. Rushu said the queen wanted it quiet, though Rysn apparently knew about it.

Everyone was pretty worried about the presence of an Oathgate out here, where who-knows-what could access it. They could keep the side at Urithiru locked, of course, so it wasn't an *immediate* danger. But still . . .

Lopen wasn't exactly certain what they were supposed to do about the thing if they did find it. He didn't have a living Blade, and neither did Huio.

He'd suggested that Kaladin send Teft along, and the answer had surprised him.

I suggested that to Navani as well, Kaladin had said. *And she replied that if this Oathgate was in the hands of enemies, she didn't fancy sending them a key. Your job is to see if it's there, scout for an enemy presence, then return. We'll decide if occupying the place is worth the difficulty after we know for certain whether the Oathgate is there.*

He stepped over to Rushu, who was doing some quick sketches of how the exoskeletons were laid out and how the gemhearts had fallen. The region felt so empty. Quiet as a home with no cousins. But after flying up a little, he could see that Huio was right; there had once been a small city at the center.

It took Lopen a while to realize something else felt eerie about the place—as if that carapace and all this unnatural silence weren't enough. No crem. Everywhere else he'd been, you could tell old things by the crem buildup. Over time, buildings became lumps in the landscape.

Not here. Nothing on the beach—the carapaces, those gemhearts—had a crust on it. No dust either. The place was, sure, cleaner than a soldier's bunk on inspection day. He lowered down and picked up a small diamond gemheart. Like the others, it wasn't glowing. He should have realized what that meant.

Highstorm water doesn't fall here, he thought, scanning the dark clouds. *Maybe the strange winds blow highstorms away?*

He tucked the gemheart in his pocket and strolled over to Rushu, then peeked over her shoulder—to her annoyance, which was fun—at the pictures she'd drawn. They were storming good, considering how quickly she'd done them.

"I once ate twelve chouta wraps in under two hours," he said to her. "It was, sure, kind of the same thing."

She gave him a baffled look. Maybe she didn't like chouta.

"Punio bet me three clearchips I couldn't do it," he explained. "So it was a matter of knightly honor."

Rushu gave him a suffering glance, then rolled and tied a little string around her drawings. She handed them to a sailor. "Take these to Brightness Rysn and tell her the beach is safe, so we'd like to continue up toward the city."

The sailor ran off and rowed with a few others to the ship. A green flag was soon raised from the mast, giving permission to continue, so Lopen gathered the assigned sailors and joined Rushu in hiking farther inland.

Huio decided to remain with the sailors on the beach, but he had a spanreed. Couldn't write with it, of course, but Huio liked to use one anyway. When you turned on the spanreed, it would make the one paired to it blink—so some Alethi officers used that to indicate a response to a message, like a raised flag.

Well, Huio took it further. Crazy chorlano. He figured he could make them blink a certain number of times to mean different things. In this case, once you noticed and acknowledged him, he had a code. One blink meant "all is well." Two meant "I'm worried." Three meant "come back immediately."

It was kind of like writing, but it was all right because it was numbers—and nobody thought numbers were unseemly for a man to use. Lopen, sure, used numbers for lots of things. He'd even made up a few. Plus Dalinar could write books, which meant everything was different now.

Lopen kept an eye on those clouds above as he walked proudly forward with Rua on his shoulder. Yes, maybe people had been here before. But that was mostly a long time ago. So . . .

"You think," he said to Rushu, "we could say I'm stepping foot on ground where no Herdazian has walked before?"

"Undoubtedly," she said. "Herdaz didn't exist when Aimia was a kingdom. Yours is a relatively new country, after all. I presume there are lots of places a person of Herdazian nationality hadn't stepped before you and the others arrived there—all of Urithiru, for example."

"Ha!" Lopen said, spinning his spear. "Stupid Huio. Come on, naco, let's go make history."

14

Rysn sat on the quiet deck of her ship, alone save for the captain and a small crew. A sailor kept watch for trouble from the eel's nest, ready to call a warning if something dangerous approached the shore team.

Rysn studied the sketches Rushu had sent. Heaps of carapace, the remnants of enormous greatshells who had died—and the gemhearts they grew. Untold riches.

It was too perfect.

Rysn looked up as she heard footsteps coming onto the quarterdeck. Cord?

"I thought you were going ashore with the dinghy, now that we know it's safe," Rysn said.

"I should go," Cord agreed. "But . . ." She looked

down over the side of the ship. "They're all below, in the water, Rysn. All of the luckspren."

"Well," Rysn said, "you could go help gather gemstones. There's heaps of treasure on that beach. Everyone who came on this mission is going to return home rich."

Cord frowned. "Yes, but he is the wrong treasure."

"You notice it too?" Rysn said.

"Notice what?"

"There's something wrong about how this looks," Rysn said, gesturing to the sketch.

"No," Cord said. "Just . . . I wanted other treasure. Shardblades and armor, like the Alethi have." Cord leaned on the railing, looking out at the beach. "My people are proud, Rysn. But we're also weak. Very weak. Not weak individually, but weak as a nation.

"We spent years and years trying to get Shards. This thing cost us many of our bravest fighters. And so far, the only Shards we have belong to my father—who insists he cannot use them." She shook her head. "The Alethi have Shards. The Thaylens have Shards. The Vedens have Shards. But on the Peaks, we have none."

"You don't need Shards, Cord," Rysn said. "You live on mountains far from everyone else. They can't get to you. And . . ."

"And they don't want to?"

"Well, yes," Rysn said. "It's nothing against you and your people. But I've made a life out of traveling to difficult places to trade, and even my babsk said that trying to trade with the Horneaters was akin to the seventh fool. I'm sure you have many things of great value, and your people seem wonderful, but the trip is so arduous that trade is almost impossible."

Cord didn't seem insulted. She simply nodded. "That's how this thing has been for many years. Nothing worth the trip . . . nothing that people knew about."

"What . . . do you mean?"

"The Alethi know now," she said. "And the enemy always knew. The Peaks have a portal, Rysn. A gateway. A path to the world of gods and spren." She met Rysn's eyes. "Soon, everyone will know. And they *will* want our land. A portal to the land of spren is valuable enough to be worth the trip to the Peaks."

"I . . ." Rysn trailed off. She wasn't certain what to make of this. A portal to the land of the spren? She'd heard about Shadesmar; rumors of it were making their way through society. But if the Horneaters had a way into the place . . .

"You are allies with the Alethi and the rest of us," Rysn said. "We can protect you."

"Pardon," Cord said. "I have Alethi friends. The

Alethi queen seems worthy. But they know that strong countries take from weak ones. They will say this thing is for everyone's good. They will say they're protecting us. But they will move to where we are. They will live in our cities. For everyone's good." She nodded. "So we must have Shards, and many Shardbearers. And Radiants—many Radiants. My father could be both. But he thinks tradition is more important than our people. I will do this thing instead. I *will* find treasures. We must be strong. So strong."

Rysn immediately felt guilty. When Cord had said she wanted treasure earlier . . . well, Rysn had assumed Cord had a simplistic, common motivation.

People talked about wealth, and how greed was such a terrible thing—and it could be dangerous, true. Yet the ambition of someone who had nothing to rise to a new station should not be easily dismissed or thought simplistic. There was so much more to it.

"So why not join the expedition going to the center of the city?" Rysn asked. "There might be Shards there."

"If there are," Cord said, "the Radiants will claim them. I need to go a different direction. And the spren . . ." She shook her head, then turned to Rysn. "Thank you, by the way."

"For . . . what?"

"For not assuming I was bad," Cord said. "That man, Nikli, he tried to . . . what is the word in Veden? Make others think I was evil?"

"He framed you."

"Framed. Like a picture?"

"Same word, different meaning."

"Ah. Why—with so many sounds—do lowlanders make words that sound the same, but mean different things? Anyway, thank you. For not believing I was evil. I think many people, they dislike foreign people like me. Always believe them to be evil. But you believed me, instead of your friend."

"I've been taught by a very wise man to see the world differently," Rysn said. "You can thank him, when I introduce you." Thinking of Vstim, however, made her realize what was bothering her about the pictures of the shore. She pointed at the sketch of the many gemhearts.

"There was a time once," Rysn said, "when I went with my babsk—the man who trained me—to trade. And the person we met had left spheres and gemstones all about, casually. A sign of wealth. My babsk, he traded differently with this person than others we'd met. Harsher, more cutthroat. Um, that means . . . well, it's another word for harsher I guess."

Cord took one of the sketches. "This thing is the same?"

"Maybe," Rysn said. "Afterward, I asked my babsk why he'd acted that way. He told me, 'People don't leave money out casually. They do it to make you see it. Either they want to pretend they have more than they have, or . . .'"

"Or?" Cord asked.

"Or they want you to fixate on it," Rysn said. "And ignore some greater prize. Would you fetch one of the sailors for me? I need to deliver a message to Rushu."

15

Lopen soared up high, Rua at his side, survey-ing the island. From up here, it seemed so small.

The city had a curious shape, like a flower with ra-diating petals. The rest of the island was boring: one big long beach. Nothing moved; nothing seemed suspicious, which he figured was how a place that *was* suspicious would act.

He dropped down to the rest of the group, where Rushu was doing a sketch of some of the buildings here at the outskirts of the city. These were covered in crem, giving them that familiar melted appear-ance that he associated with old things.

"From up there," he said, "it all just looks like rocks. Why do you suppose there's crem here, but not on the beach?"

"I would guess," she said, still sketching, "that

some of this was already covered in crem when the highstorms stopped reaching this island. The carapace and gemhearts by the beach are certainly old, but they must be fresher than these ruins."

What he'd mistaken for walls when first approaching was really a line of buildings. Homes, perhaps? They were uniform, and groups of them formed the "tips" of the flower petals he'd seen from above.

Rushu finished her sketch, then turned to another page in her notebook—one that contained some kind of map.

"Hey!" Lopen said. "That looks exactly like the city!"

"An ancient map of Akinah," she explained. "I was hoping to use it to conclusively prove this is the same place. You seem to have done that for me."

"Glad to help," Lopen said. With their squad of eight spear-wielding sailors, they moved inward, passing the grown-over buildings and entering the heart of the city.

Here, the roofs had all fallen in, leaving pillars and some remnants of walls. It was covered in just enough crem to make the ruins feel like they were sinking into the ground, but not enough to turn them into lumps. The result gave the place an almost *rotting* cast, reminding him of the refuse he'd find in the chasms with Bridge Four. These were the bones, the broken branches, and the withered flesh of a once grand city.

"It's smaller than I'd imagined," Lopen said, turning about and using his spear to gesture toward the far end of the city. "I could walk across the whole place in, sure, less time than it takes Punio to do his hair before we go out dancing."

"Older cities were all that way," Rushu said. "It was harder for the ancients to build windbreaks and aqueducts, and they didn't have large trade operations to resupply cities with food. So everything was constructed on a much smaller scale."

Lopen turned around in a circle, feeling like those broken buildings were skulls, with sunken eye sockets for windows, all dripping with hardened crem. Rushu sent the sailors to go searching through some of those, and he shivered. Why was he so nervous about this place?

"I . . . don't know that we'll find anything useful in here, Rushu," he said, scanning about. "The place is less ruins than rubble."

"The fact that it exists in such an undisturbed state is *monumentally* important, Lopen," Rushu said. "It will be of great interest to archaeologists and historians. The more we've learned about the Recreance, the more we've realized that our understanding of the past is painfully incomplete."

"I suppose," Lopen said as she held up her little map. "Any idea where the Oathgate would be?"

"Well, the optimal place would be in the center of the city for equilateral access," Rushu said. "Either that, or nearest the docks for maximum trade convenience. Unfortunately, judging by the three in Azimir, Kholinar, and Thaylen City, the Oathgates were *not* placed optimally. Instead, all three are within convenient access of the ruling class."

"Storming lighteyes," Lopen muttered. "Always making things more difficult for us common folk."

"Us common folk?" she asked. "You are a Knight Radiant."

"The most common one."

"You frequently tell me how uncommon you are, Lopen."

"It's only a contradiction if you think about it."

"I . . . I have no response to that."

"See? You are getting it already. So . . . where would the rich folks have been in this city?"

"My guess is those larger lumps over there. The Oathgates tend to be on large platforms, and that section seems to be raised higher than the surroundings."

They began walking toward the ruins she had indicated. As they did, Lopen found himself holding his spear tightly and checking over his shoulder. And storms, it wasn't just him being jumpy. There was something unnerving about this place. With those clouds overhead, the distant fog, the stillness.

It was, sure, a mausoleum. But instead of being for kings or such, it was for an entire people. This had once been a vibrant capital, a center of trade.

It wasn't simply ruins. It was *lonely* ruins, always overcast and never seeing the sun, but also never seeing rain or storm. Was that why Rysn's porter had worked so hard to keep them away? To prevent them from disturbing the place's slumber? Or had Lopen listened to one too many of Rock's firelight stories about spirits and gods?

At any rate, he nearly jumped all the way to the Halls when someone came around the corner. Lopen yelled and drew in Stormlight, then felt foolish. It was only Pluv, one of the sailors.

"Message for Ardent Rushu," he said, "from the *rebsk*."

Rushu took the note and read it while Lopen scanned the ruins again. He spotted all eight sailors, and a part of him was surprised that one hadn't vanished mysteriously. He ought to go tell them to stick together, just in case.

"Curious," Rushu said, tucking away the note.

"What does she say?"

"It's a warning," Rushu said. "She thinks everything about this place is too expected, too perfect. An opening in the stones out in the water, leading toward a perfect landing beach, with gemstones littered around for the taking? I suppose even these ruins are exactly as I imagined them. . . ."

"So what does it mean?" Lopen asked.

"I'm not sure. Did you, by chance, grab any of those gemstones on the beach?"

Lopen fished in his pocket for the small gemheart he'd picked up earlier. "Grabbed one," he said. "I was going to ask you what you thought about there being no crem on it, but got distracted."

She took it from his fingers, then brought out a jeweler's loupe and began inspecting it.

"You . . . carry one of those in your pocket?" Lopen asked.

"Doesn't everyone?" she said absently. "Hmm. I can't be certain, as I'm no expert. But I think . . . Lopen, I think this is a fake. Quartz, not a diamond."

He frowned, taking it back. Quartz couldn't hold Stormlight, and it could be made by a Soulcaster. "You think . . . they might all be fakes?"

"It's possible."

Lopen gave a mighty sigh. "And thus, my great fortune evaporates like a man's beauty upon the weathering shores of time. Like how that one time I, sure, almost had a chasmfiend pet that would—"

"Yes, you've told me," Rushu said. "Six times."

"I have a new joke though," Lopen said. "For the end of the story. I'm going to say, 'And that is why I let it eat my arm.' Funny, yes? Well, it will be. Eventually." He tossed the fake gemheart up in the air and caught it again. "So . . . why make these? Why set this place up to appear so rich?"

"I'm wondering the same thing," Rushu said.

"They wanted to wow us, maybe?" Lopen said. "Perhaps they thought we'd be so distracted by the riches that we'd be stunned and confused. They did not know that I am accustomed to such incredible sights, for I experience something even more impressive each morning after I awake."

"Is that so?"

"When I look in the mirror."

"And you wonder why you're still single."

"Oh, I don't wonder," he said. "I'm fully aware that so much of me is difficult for any one woman to handle. My majesty confuses them. It's the only explanation for why they often run away." He gave her a grin.

Surprisingly, she grinned back. Usually people threw things at him when he said lines like that.

She led him the rest of the way to the raised section of the city, which did kind of look like an Oathgate platform. She pointed to a structure in the near distance that looked like it might have been a palace.

"If this is like Kholinar," she said, "then . . ."

They turned and walked to a solitary structure—one of the few that still had a roof—near the center of the raised platform. Inside, they found what they'd been searching for. Kind of.

This had obviously once been an Oathgate chamber. It had the remnants of the same mural on the floor as the ones in other cities, but the mechanism had broken or decayed. There was no place to put a Shardblade, no way to rotate it. The structure had been destroyed by the elements. All that remained was dust and corroded bits of metal.

Lopen frowned, picking up some of these and feeling them with his thumb. He glanced at Rushu, who stood with her hands on her hips, her forehead wrinkled in thought. Something about this place felt wrong. Like it . . . like it had lodged in his throat as he tried to swallow it. And he couldn't get it down. He had to cough it back up instead.

"This is fake too, isn't it?" he said.

"What makes you say that?" Rushu asked.

"Well, the Oathgate on the Shattered Plains sat there, sure, for thousands of years—and it still worked when we found it. This place is better preserved. But here, the Oathgate mechanism has disintegrated?"

"I agree," she said. "I might have bought it, but

those gemstones . . . And then finding this next to the palace, like in Kholinar? It's too obvious."

"So where's the real one?" Lopen asked.

"Go fetch the sailors," she said. "See if they can locate a set of stairs. Or a trapdoor. Or anything in this rubble that would let us go down."

That seemed strange to Lopen. People didn't often build *down*, since basements tended to fill with water. Still, Rushu was a smart one, so he shouldered his spear and walked out to do as she asked. He gathered the sailors and had them, in pairs, start searching for steps.

He couldn't banish that feeling of *wrongness* as they did so, and he kept seeing things at the corners of his eyes. Storm him, but this place had him jumping at shadows.

But Rushu was right. It didn't take too long before they found a stairwell hidden by some debris in one of the least impressive buildings on the outskirts of the central plaza, not particularly close to the palace at all.

"It's probably a stormcellar," Lopen said, following Rushu down and holding a gemstone for light.

"Probably," she agreed.

"Or . . ." he said as they reached the bottom, "it's just a dead end." Indeed, the stairwell ended abruptly at a stone wall.

Rushu took a small pouch off her belt, one that clinked as she moved it.

"Why did you want us to find steps anyway?" Lopen asked.

"It's not uncommon for ancient cities to be buried over time," she said. "Crem builds up. While modern cities keep chipping at it to prevent being swallowed, many older towns were built on top of the submerged ruins of ancient ones. It's not uncommon to discover an architectural site when digging a mine, for example."

"All right . . ." Lopen said. "So . . ."

"So I have double the reason to believe that city above is fake," she said. "The real Akinah probably sank into the crem years ago." She held out her hand—which glowed suddenly with a fierce light. The ardent wore gemstones on it, connected with silver chains.

"Storms!" he said. "A Soulcaster?"

"Yes," she said. "Let me see if I can remember how to use one of these. . . ."

"You know *how*?"

"Of course," she said. "The Soulcasting ardents use them all the time. I went through a phase when I was *very* keen on joining them, until I discovered how boring their work was. Anyway, plug your ears and hold your breath."

"Why—"

He cut off as smoke *filled* the stairwell, making his ears scream with sudden pressure, as if he'd dived deep beneath the ocean. He shouted, then coughed. Then drew in some Stormlight.

Ahead of him, the stone wall had vanished. Rushu was wiping the soot from her face with a rag and grinning.

"You're crazy," he told her.

"Well, I suspected that if an Oathgate *was* here in Akinah, we'd have to cut through stone to get to it. I didn't anticipate this one being underground—more that it would be covered over like on the Shattered Plains. Regardless, I demanded that Navani send me with either a Shardblade or a Soulcaster to get through. Alas, she picked the less exciting option. I do like being right though. It makes my stomach flutter."

Lopen stepped up beside her, holding out his gemstone to reveal what she'd opened up. An underground cavern, somewhat shallow—maybe twelve feet high—and expansively wide. Like . . . a plateau.

"Storms," Lopen said. "The Oathgate *is* down here."

"It must have taken extraordinary effort to hide it," Rushu said. "Whoever did this could have simply buried it, but they wanted to leave it functional.

So they built a room around it, then let the crem pile up over the years."

"But why?" Lopen asked, stepping into the place, squinting. His light barely revealed the control building at the center. Yes, this really was an Oathgate. "Why hide it, then go to all that trouble to construct fake buildings?"

"Obviously," Rushu said, "they hoped we'd find the fake one, then leave, assuming the Oathgate lost."

Lopen halted in place. The words sank in. This idea he swallowed, but it tasted terrible.

"This was like . . . a failsafe," he whispered. "So if someone reached the island, they'd find nothing useful."

"But we outthought them!" Rushu said. "I'll have to remember to thank Brightness Rysn for her timely note. It—"

"Rushu," Lopen interrupted, fishing out the gemstone Huio had given him. It wasn't blinking. "You're a genius."

"Clearly."

"But you're also a storming fool. Gather the sailors, stay here, and try not to get killed." With that, he went dashing back up the steps, pulling in Stormlight. He took to the air immediately, zipping out of the city and toward the beach.

Whoever was watching this place, they'd gone

to great lengths to prevent them from arriving. But once that plan had been foiled, they'd probably been willing to let the expedition gather up fake gemhearts and sail away. So long as they didn't find the real secret of the island.

But he and Rushu had done just that. Which meant the entire group was in serious danger, even if Huio's gemstone wasn't blinking. He needed to get to the others quickly.

He was glad for his instincts. Because when he arrived at the beach, he found Huio being eaten by a monster. And that wasn't the sort of event a cousin should miss.

Rysn's first clue came as a curious sound. A clicking, like moving carapace?

She'd been waiting for a rowboat to return to take her to join the shore team. She wanted to inspect the greatshell remains there, see if she could spot anything that gave her a clue on how to help Chiri-Chiri. Now, she turned around in her seat on the quarterdeck and looked toward the strange sound. Had Chiri-Chiri returned?

But no. This sound she was hearing was too loud to be made by one creature. It was . . . the sound of *hundreds* of legs moving at once.

What she saw in the water made her feel as if

she'd been struck by a bolt of lightning. Hundreds of cremlings—crustaceans smaller than a person's fist—were crawling out of the ocean and up the side of the ship. And each seemed to be carrying a piece of *flesh* on it. She even spotted one with an eyeball on its back.

Had these things ripped apart a person? Were they carrion feeders? Something worse?

She screamed, but did so a fraction too late to be of help—for a shout went up across the ship's deck. Sailors on watch called out as the water around the *Wandersail* boiled, spitting out thousands of similar cremlings. Clacking and chittering and scrambling as they swarmed up the sides of the ship.

Violet fearspren gathered at Rysn's feet. Never before had she felt more trapped by her inability to walk. Cord muttered something in Horneater and backed away. Rysn, however, had to unstrap herself before she could escape.

She was too slow. Her trembling fingers didn't seem to work as she fought with the buckles. The strange cremlings flooded over the side railing.

She finally got the belt undone, but by then the things were swarming all around her. She couldn't flop onto the deck and crawl away. She'd be overrun. Instead she tried to pull herself farther up into the seat.

However, instead of crawling up her legs and attacking her, some of the cremlings pooled on the deck nearby. Then, in a bizarre display, they began to *fit together*. Like people grabbing hands and forming a line, the cremlings interlocked their wriggling legs, putting their backs outward. The bits of flesh and skin on them fit together like pieces of a puzzle.

Humanlike feet formed, then legs. Cremlings crawled up, pulling together into a writhing heap that became a torso—then finally the full figure of a nude man, lacking genitals. The head came last, eyes popping into place as cremlings squeezed inside the "skull." Lines of tattoos hid the seams in the skin.

For a moment, the look of it was nauseating— the figure's stomach pulsed with the creatures moving within. Lumps twitched on the arms. The skin of the legs split as if sliced open, revealing the insectile horrors within. Then it all seemed to *tighten* and settle down, and appeared human. A near-perfect likeness, though the lines across the stomach and thighs were far more visible than the ones on the hands and face.

"Hello, Rysn," Nikli said. He smiled, and his face creased along lines she now knew weren't merely wrinkles, but splits in the skin. "Your expedition has, unfortunately, proven very persistent."

Storms. Nikli wasn't a man or a Voidbringer. He

was something worse: one of the gods from Cord's stories, a monster from Jasnah's tales. An abomination made up of hundreds of tiny pieces pretending to be a single entity.

Cord put her hand on Rysn's shoulder—making her jump—then stepped deliberately forward to position herself between Nikli and Rysn. The Horneater woman spoke in her musical language, and the creature—remarkably—responded in kind.

"Cord?" Rysn whispered, trembling. "What is happening?"

"I did not realize . . ." Cord whispered in Veden. "The Gods Who Sleep Not . . . they can appear as people."

"Do you know how to fight one?"

"I told you, you cannot," Cord said. "Lunu'anaki—he is trickster god—warned of them during my grandmother's time when she was the watcher of the pool."

"We had not expected to find one of the Sighted on this trip," Nikli said in Veden. "You have long guarded Cultivation's Perpendicularity. It is regrettable that you joined this expedition. We do not kill your people lightly, Hualinam'lunanaki'akilu."

Some of the other swarms formed into similar individuals on the deck, though several remained scuttling masses. The captain gathered the remaining ten or so sailors, but they were quickly surrounded by the strange creatures. Storms. The men had grabbed spears, but how did you fight something like this? One man stabbed a creature that drew close, and the spear stuck straight through the body, then cremlings began to swarm out of the body cavity along the spear's length.

"Stop this," Rysn said, finding her voice. "Nikli, let us negotiate. Please, tell me what you want."

"All opportunity for negotiation has passed," Nikli said softly, looking away—a very humanlike gesture of shame. "You ignored my warnings, and your friends on the island did not take the bait we offered them. That was your last chance to escape safely, and some of us argued long to give you even that chance.

"But you are persistent, as I said. Some of us knew it would come to this. Some who are less idealistic than I. For what it is worth, Rysn, I'm sorry. I genuinely enjoyed our time together. But the very cosmere is at stake. A few deaths now, however regrettable, will prevent catastrophe."

Cord shouted something at Nikli in Horneater, and he retorted, sounding angry, then turned to shout toward the others on the deck.

"That was a distraction," Cord whispered to Rysn, turning. "Be ready. Hold your breath."

"Hold my—"

Rysn yelped as Cord grabbed her around the waist. The tall woman heaved Rysn over her shoulder, leaped onto the chair, then launched them over the side of the ship toward the dark waters beyond.

16

For a moment, Rysn was transported back to the Reshi Isles.

Falling.

Falling.

Hitting water.

For a moment she was in that deep again, after having plunged from such an incredible height. Numb. Watching the light retreat. Unable to move. Unable to save herself.

Then the two moments separated. She wasn't in the Reshi Isles; she was in the frigid ocean near Akinah. The shock of the cold made her want to gasp or scream. Fortunately, she kept her mouth closed as Cord—swimming mostly with her legs—propelled them downward.

Deeper.

Deeper.

Fearspren trailed behind Rysn like bubbles. Cord was an unexpectedly powerful swimmer. But being carried this way, pulled into the dark, made Rysn panic. It brought back not only the terror of her near-death experience, but the helplessness of the awful weeks that had followed.

Previously mundane acts—like getting out of bed, visiting the washroom, or even getting herself something to eat—had suddenly become near-impossible. The resulting fear, frustration, and helplessness had almost overwhelmed Rysn. She'd spent days lying in bed, feeling that she should have died rather than becoming such a burden.

She had surmounted those emotions. With effort, and help from her parents and Vstim, she'd realized there was so much she could still do. She *could* make her life better. She was *not* a burden. She was a person.

However, as the ocean swallowed her again, she found her old fears alive and well, festering inside. The abject sense of helplessness. The terror at being entirely at the mercy of other people.

And then she saw the spren.

Not the fearspren, but luckspren—like arrowheads with stubby, rippling bodies. They darted through the water around her and Cord. Dozens. Hundreds. Light from the clouded sky above vanished, and Rysn's ears hurt so much she was forced to equalize by blowing with her nose pinched.

But those spren were glowing, lighting the way, urging them forward.

I know you, spren, she thought. She should have panicked, should have worried about drowning. Instead she watched the spren. *How did I fall from so high and not die? Everyone called it a miracle....*

She twisted in Cord's grip. The spren led them toward a shimmering light emanating from some rocks ahead. A small tunnel?

At last Rysn noticed her lungs beginning to burn. She slipped out of Cord's grasp and turned, then pulled herself along the rocks. Cord came behind, and the spren ushered them, guided them through the dark depths until—

Rysn pulled herself up into the air. Cord emerged a moment later.

Rysn gasped for breath, trembling in the darkness. What had happened to the light? The spren? Suddenly it was completely dark, though the sound of their breath echoed against nearby walls. They seemed to have emerged into some kind of cavern under the island.

Rysn grabbed some rocks at the side of the pool, clinging to them with her right arm as she reached to the money pouch in her left skirt pocket for spheres. She fiddled in it, then brought out a bright diamond mark, gripping it through the thin cloth of her safehand glove.

The light revealed Cord, her red hair plastered to her skin, holding to the rocks nearby. They were indeed in a cavern—well, a tunnel that ended in a small pool.

Cord climbed up onto the rocks, then helped Rysn out. They sat for a moment, coughing, breathing deeply.

"Are they still here?" Rysn eventually asked. "The luckspren?"

"*Apaliki'tokoa'a,*" Cord said, pointing in the air, though Rysn saw nothing. "They appeared to you?"

"Yes," Rysn whispered. "Under the water."

"They guided us, sped us as we swam..." Cord said. "My father has always had the blessings of spren. They used to strengthen his arm, when he drew the Bow of Hours in the Peaks, but I've never known such blessings." Her finger traced a path leading down the tunnel. "They are going this way."

"The creatures that came onto the ship," Rysn said. "Nikli...whatever he is. They can swim. I doubt we're safe down here."

"Perhaps there is a way out," Cord said. "I will look?"

Rysn nodded, though she didn't have much hope. During her travels with her babsk, they'd visited the Purelake, where he'd made her read a book on the local people. There had been an entire chapter on how the place drained during storms, and though she hadn't been able to make much sense of it, she was pretty certain a chamber this far down couldn't have air unless there was no way for it to escape upward.

That meant they were cornered. Rysn settled her back against a stone, her legs stretched in front of her. Cord hurried off, dripping water and carrying a sphere for light. Rysn fished in her pockets. What did she have of use? A few more spheres and some ruby fabrials?

For a moment, she thought they were from spanreeds. But no, these were the rubies from her chair, secured in metal housings with straps to tie them into place. They were paired with a set on the anchor rigged to the mast of the ship.

Strange, to think how optimistic she'd been only a short time ago. Before she'd led the entire crew to their doom. Would Radiants Lopen and Huio be able to save them, maybe?

And so you're helpless again? she thought. *Just sitting around, waiting for someone else to come and take care of you?*

Vstim had put her in command for a reason. He trusted her. Couldn't she do herself the same honor?

"Rysn!" Cord called, her voice echoing in the tunnel. The Horneater woman appeared a short time later, panting, her eyes wide. Her figure threw crazy shadows across the walls as she waved the hand holding the sphere. "You must see!"

"See what?" Rysn asked.

"*Treasure*," Cord said. "Plate, Rysn. *Shardplate*. The gods heard my prayers and have led me to him!" She stooped to heave Rysn over her shoulder again.

"Wait," Rysn said. "Let's try these, maybe?" She held up a ruby and activated it with a twist of part of the housing. That left it hanging in the air.

Cord ran off, then returned shortly with a small bench and an antiquated spear. That worked fairly well; using the leather straps on the fabrials, Rysn tied them to the legs of the small bench. When Cord lifted the bench and Rysn activated the fabrials, they made it hover. It did rise and fall slightly with the movements of the ship up above, but with the still ocean around here, that variation wasn't much.

A short time later, Rysn poled herself through the air with the spear, hovering alongside Cord. Though the place where they'd emerged had been unworked stone, the next section of the tunnel had been carved into a corridor. On its walls they found strange murals. People with hands forward, falling through what appeared to be portals, emerging into . . . light?

Not far past these, they entered a small room. It was perhaps fifteen feet square, and Rysn's eyes were immediately drawn to the incredible mural that dominated the far wall. It depicted a sun being shattered into pieces.

Cord showed her the set of Shardplate, which had been carefully piled in one corner of the small chamber, along with some ornate weapons and clothing. None of those seemed to be Shardweapons, but . . . those were *Soulcaster* devices, arranged in little boxes by the wall. Four were on a bench identical to the one Rysn floated upon, and four were on the ground, probably moved by Cord.

A metal door set into the stone at the left side of the room was cracked slightly open. Rysn poled herself over and peeked through to see an even larger corridor, this one with a vaulted ceiling and fine worked stone walls. Light shimmered somewhere farther along it, illuminating large carapace skulls with deep black eye sockets.

Though she was tempted to continue exploring, something about the grand mural in the small room drew Rysn back. She poled over to it as Cord attempted to activate the Shardplate—not a bad idea, considering their situation. Cord asked her for gemstones, and Rysn absently handed over her sphere pouch.

That mural . . . it was circular and—inlaid with golden foil—it seemed to glow with its own light. The writing on parts of it was unfamiliar to Rysn; she hadn't seen the script during any of her travels. It wasn't even the Dawnchant.

The peculiar letters were art themselves, curling around the outside of the exploding sun—which was divided into mostly symmetrical pieces. Four of them, each in turn broken into four smaller sections.

Her spear slipped from her fingers and clattered to the floor. She swore she could feel the *heat* of that sun, burning, washing over her. It was not angry, though she knew it was being ripped apart like a person on some awful torture device.

She felt something emanating from it. Resignation? Confidence? *Understanding?*

This is the real treasure, she thought, although she didn't know why. *Those words. Burning on the wall.*

Who had created this? She had never experienced such grandeur. She traced the pieces of breaking sunlight with her eyes. Gold foil on the inside. Red foil tracing the outer lines to give them depth and definition. She counted the shards in her mind, over and over, feeling a reverence to the number. The sun *held* her.

You were brought here, she thought to herself, *by one of the Guardians of Ancient Sins.*

Of course she had been. That made sense.

Wait. Did it?

Yes, she thought. *You were. There are few of them left. And so the Sleepless take up the task.*

Naturally. All that nonsense on the surface of the island? Distractions. Intended to keep anyone from looking for this.

Rysn shook herself, tearing her eyes away from the mural. Those had felt like someone else's thoughts intruding into her mind. What was happening to her? Why had she dropped her spear? After all that work to be able to move on her own, she'd simply let go?

She reached down, but she was too far up in the air. As she leaned over, she felt a *pressure* on her mind. The mural. Calling to her.

Nearby, Cord muttered softly. Rysn glanced over to find the Horneater woman had the Shardplate boots on, and was now trying to force the breastplate to take her spheres.

"I think you need free gemstones, Cord," Rysn said. "Not ones encased in glass."

"I don't have enough of those," Cord said.

"We could use these." Rysn gestured to the rubies under her bench.

Cord hesitated.

"It's all right," Rysn said. "If you can get that Plate working, you might be able to defend us."

Cord nodded, striding over to help Rysn down. She felt . . . regretful. Every time she had a taste of freedom, something happened to steal it away from her.

Cord sat Rysn on the cold stones, then pried the four rubies from their housings. She hooked them into the greaves of the Plate, which she then attached to her legs. They tightened immediately, locking into place.

She glanced at the breastplate. "We need more."

Rysn pointed to the cracked door on the other side of the room. "I saw light that direction, in the larger tunnel. Maybe gemstones?"

Cord rushed over and pulled open the door, looking past the enormous carapace skulls toward the distant light. "There are spren," Cord said, then began walking that way, her metal boots clomping on the ground. She carried the breastplate with her, though it seemed extremely heavy.

Rysn turned, trying not to look at the wall, which was growing even warmer. Unfortunately, she soon heard splashes coming from the direction of the pool. Their enemy had found them.

Guardian of Ancient Sins, she thought. What did that mean? Why did the idea repeat over and over in her mind?

She felt the mural looming. Overshadowing her. Slowly, she turned and gazed up at the exploding sun.

Accept it.

Know it.

CHANGE.

It stilled, waiting. Waiting for . . .

"Yes," Rysn whispered.

Something slammed into her mind. It streamed from the mural through her eyes, searing her skull. It gripped her, held to her, *joined* with her. Light consumed Rysn entirely.

A moment later, she found herself panting on the ground. She blinked, then felt at her eyes. Though tears leaked from the corners, her skin wasn't on fire, and she hadn't been blinded. She glanced up at the mural and noted it was unchanged. Except . . . she no longer felt warmth from it. It was only a mural. Beautiful, yes, but no longer . . .

No longer what? What had changed?

Scuttling sounds. Hundreds of little footsteps on the stone coming from behind. She twisted and grabbed the spear that she'd been using to move earlier, but she was no soldier.

So what was she? Useless?

No, she thought, determined never to sink into that self-pity again. *I am far from useless.*

It was time to prove she deserved Vstim's trust.

17

L open zipped straight toward the giant sea monster. It looked vaguely like an enormous grub with a wicked beak of a face. It had spindly arms running all the way along its body, and had reared up so it was mostly vertical, using its pointed limbs like spears to try to skewer the sailors beneath.

Huio was literally inside the thing's mouth, holding its mandibles apart with a spear, barely preventing himself from being crushed. So Lopen was able to soar up and grab Huio by the arm, then tow him out of the way. The thing snapped its mouth closed behind them, breaking the spear with an awful *crack*.

Sailors huddled in the skulls on the beach, using the carapace as cover, clutching spears and cowering before the monster. It was as tall as a building, swarming with arrowhead luckspren. Lopen pulled to a stop in the air, holding Huio. The cousins met one another's eyes.

Then Huio groaned. "I'm never going to hear the end of this, am I?"

"Ha!" Lopen said. "You were going to get *eaten*! You were going to be swallowed by a giant monster that looks like something you'd step on during worming season!"

"Can we focus on the fight?"

"Hey, have you heard about the time I saved Huio from being swallowed? Oh yes. He was going to get eaten. By a monster uglier than the women he courts. And I flew *into* the thing's mouth to save him. Off the tongue. Then I was very humble about having done such a heroic deed."

"Leave that last part off," Huio said. "It will make them easily discern that you are lying." He breathed in, borrowing Stormlight from Lopen's spheres. "Watch out. There are some cremlings around here that steal Stormlight."

"Is it the one the boss-lady had?"

"No, smaller," Huio said, Lashing himself so he hovered in the air. "And of a different breed. I didn't get a good look, but I think they flew around in a little swarm."

Huio swooped down and snatched a new spear

off the ground. Lopen raised his, glancing at Rua, who had changed shape to mimic that of the monster. He bounced around growling. The monster turned toward them and swiped with a spearlike limb, causing a rush of wind as Lopen ducked it.

"You know," Lopen said to Rua, "now would be an excellent time for you to decide that you'd like to be a Shardblade."

Rua wagged a crustacean finger at him. An annoyed gesture that conveyed, "You know you have to earn that."

"I will protect even those I hate," Lopen said. "See? I can say it." He dodged again. "It's easy."

Rua-monster wagged another limb.

"But *I* don't hate *anyone*!" Lopen complained. "And nobody hates me. I'm The Lopen. How could they? These rules, sure, aren't fair!"

Rua-monster shrugged.

"You used to be on my side on this one, naco," Lopen grumbled. "This is Phendorana's fault, isn't it? You shouldn't listen to her lectures."

This probably wasn't the time for such a conversation. They had a monster to defeat. Spear in hand, Lopen swooped in to distract it as it tried to go after some of the sailors.

* * *

Rysn arranged herself meticulously. She pulled over the bench she'd been sitting on earlier and placed it in front of her. It was a little too high and thin to be a Thaylen merchant's deal table, but it was a reasonable approximation.

If you wanted to deal in the traditional way, you sat on mats on the floor, opposite the table from one another. She managed to get her legs crossed, her back to the wall with the mural to help prop herself up.

She put her hands palm down on the table in the formal dealing posture and tried to remember her lessons.

The creatures came in along the walls and ceiling. They swarmed in that same nauseating way: heaps of cremlings snapping together into something that imitated a human, but with distressing lumps shifting under the "skin."

Soon Nikli stood in front of her.

Rysn controlled her trembling as best she could, ignoring the fearspren, then turned her hands palm upward. "This," she said, "is the traditional sign inviting the initiation of a trade deal between two Thaylen merchants. I'm not sure how much of our culture you picked up during your time imitating a human."

"I picked up enough," Nikli said, stepping forward. Two other figures remained behind. One might have been imitating a male, the other a female, though it was hard to tell. Nikli picked up a robe draped across a few spears in the pile of armor, then pulled it on. "I'm young among my people, but I have lived quite a long time. I sailed with Longbrow, you know. I liked him, for all his boasting."

Storms. Longbrow was four hundred years dead. Rysn steeled herself. *Oh, storms.* She was swimming in water far over her head. And there was still that strange heat in the back of her mind. The pressure. The *Command.*

She gestured toward the other side of the table. "Sit. Let us negotiate."

"There is nothing to negotiate, Rysn," Nikli said. "I'm sorry. But I have a duty to the entire cosmere."

"Everyone wants something," Rysn said, sweat trickling down the sides of her face. "Everyone has needs. It is my job to connect the needs to the people."

"And what is it you assume I need?" Nikli asked.

She met the thing's gaze. "You need someone to keep your secrets."

18

H ey, Huio," Lopen shouted. "I was wrong about this monster resembling the women you court. It actually looks like you in the mornings, before you've had your ornachala!"

A leg speared down near Lopen, tossing up chips of rock as it struck the ground.

"Acts like you too!" Lopen said, Lashing himself backward. Mostly he was keeping the beast's attention. He wanted it focused on him and Huio, not the sailors. Indeed, because of Huio's efforts earlier, it looked like only one sailor had been seriously injured so far. Fimkn was trying to bind the man's wounds while the rest had grabbed an extra stock of spears from the rowboats. The men proved adept with the weapons, throwing them to try to stick them in the creature's eyes. One got close, bouncing off the carapace right near an eye.

The thing roared and reared up, a giant pink-white tube of death covered in carapace. Though the dozen or so arms seemed spindly by comparison, they were thick as tree trunks. They alternated between trying to spear Lopen and trying to swat him from the sky.

Lopen wiped his brow, then ordered the sailors to back up farther ashore. Unfortunately, while the creature seemed like it belonged in the water, it was mobile enough on the shore to be dangerous, using its legs to scoot along, sluglike.

It turned toward the sailors again, so Lopen buzzed in close, Rua at his side, and drew its attention. He tried spearing the thing in the head near the neck, but his weapon bounced off. The monster was bulbous like a grub, but far better armored.

Damnation. Lopen Lashed himself and wove between its swinging arms. Ha! At least it was slow-moving like a grub. The thing could barely—

WHAM.

Lopen ended up sprawled against a boulder, upside down, ribs screaming as they knit back together with Stormlight.

"Radiant Lopen!" Kstled said, ducking in close. "Are you all right?"

"Feel like a piece of snot," Lopen said, groaning, "following a sneeze." He peeled himself off the rock and flopped down next to Kstled. "My spear can't get through that thing's carapace."

"We need a Shardblade!" Kstled said. "Can't you summon one?"

"Afraid not," Lopen said. "It's political." Nearby, Huio was drawing the thing's attention, but his Stormlight was waning. "Don't get eaten again!" Lopen called. "But if you do, try not to get sneezed out! It's *awful*!"

"Political?" Kstled asked.

"You've got to say these words," Lopen said, "and I said them, because they're good words. But the Stormfather, sure, he has no sense of style." He glanced up at the sky. "This would be a great time, O blustery one! I will protect those I hate! I've got it, you den gancho god thing!"

No response.

Lopen sighed, then shouldered his spear. "All right, so Huio and I will try to lead it farther inland. Then you and your sailors, sure, you grab those boats and try to get to the ship."

"We can't let it follow us to the *Wandersail*!" Kstled said. "A greatshell like that could sink the ship!"

"Yeah, well, then we need to *all* retreat and try

to lead it inward. We can maybe take shelter in the buildings inland!"

"What if in running, we encourage it to move out and attack the ship?"

"We'll just have to deal with that if it happens, all right? Huio and I will distract it; the rest of you prepare to retreat up to the fallen city."

Kstled hesitated, then nodded. Lopen Lashed himself into the air and shot toward the thing. Maybe if he could get in close while it was focused on Huio, he could stab it real good. He also needed to give Huio some more Stormlight. Lopen had plenty, sure, in his pouches.

He flew around behind the thing, but it seemed ready for this. It kept shifting, keeping one of its beady jet-black eyes toward Lopen while it slammed its arms toward Huio.

Huio shouted at it, fortunately drawing its attention. *There!* Lopen thought, preparing his spear. He got in closer. When it glanced toward him again, he'd Lash the spear directly into its eye.

Lopen felt a sudden chill.

A coldness began at his back, right between his shoulder blades, then washed through him. Cold enough that it made him jerk upright, stunned. Unable to move as he felt something *leeched* from him.

His Stormlight.

He managed to spin in the air, trying to swing his spear and attack. But it was too late. He glimpsed a swarm of small cremlings flying behind him—different from the one Rysn had as a pet. Smaller—maybe the size of his fist—and more bulbous, the two dozen creatures barely managed to hang in the air. But their feeding had been enough to drain him.

As he dropped through the air, he felt panic. They'd gotten his pouches too. There was nothing left to suck in. He—

He hit. *Hard.* Something snapped in his leg.

The monster undulated toward him, opening its awful maw and glaring with those terrible eyes. It seemed eager as it raised its arms to smash him.

You were there when I met Navani Kholin," Rysn said to Nikli. "You know she isn't the type to be easily dissuaded."

"The Mother of Machines," Nikli said it like a distinctive title. "Yes. We are . . . aware."

"You tried to scare away her Windrunners when they investigated this island," Rysn said, "so she sent a ship. What do you think will happen if that ship vanishes mysteriously? You think she'll give up? You'll see a fleet next."

Nikli sighed, then met her eyes. "You assume we don't have plans in place, Rysn," he said. He seemed genuine. Though he was made up of monsters inside, he appeared to be the person she'd come to know during their travels.

"Your plans so far haven't worked," Rysn said. "Why would you assume one to scare off the Radiants will?"

"I . . . I wish you'd taken our bait," he said. "Some of us wanted to sink your ship as soon as it breached the storm. But we persuaded them. We told them you'd be happy with the gemhearts. You were supposed to also locate a little stash of maps and writings from long ago; we would have made sure you found it before leaving.

"Once you returned to Queen Navani, you'd have discovered that the gemhearts were fake. The writings would prove to be the remnants of an old pirate scheme, from the days before this place was surrounded with a storm. You'd have learned those pirates used legends of treasure to lure people to Akinah—that they'd spread fake gemstones on the beaches to draw their marks in and distract them before attacking.

"It would have been so neat, so easy. With those stories in hand, everyone would dismiss the legends about riches on Akinah. They'd leave us alone. No one would have to die. Except . . ."

"Except there's an Oathgate here," Rysn said. "They'll never leave it alone, Nikli."

"They will think it destroyed," Nikli said. "After . . . what must regrettably be done here to you and your crew . . . some of us will imitate sailors. Your ship will limp back to port, and we will tell the story. A storm that cost too many lives while getting through it. A fight with a strange greatshell. A destroyed Oathgate. Fake gemhearts. Everyone will leave us alone after that."

Damnation. That might work.

But Vstim's calm voice seemed to whisper to her from across the ocean. This was her moment. The most important deal of her life. What did they want? What did they *say* they wanted?

Storms, I'm not ready for something like this, she thought.

You'll have to do it anyway.

She took a deep breath. "You truly think you can imitate my ship's sailors well enough to fool people who knew them? You use a body with tattoos, I assume to hide the seams in your skin. You don't quite know how to act Thaylen, so you imitate a foreigner. You actually think this subterfuge will work? Or will it instead spread *more* mystery?"

Nikli met her eyes, but didn't reply.

"That's been your problem all along," Rysn said. "Each lie you spin makes the mystery more entrancing. You want to protect this place. What if I could help you?"

Rysn's mouth had gone dry. But she continued holding the creature's eyes. No, *Nikli's* eyes. She had to see him as the person she knew. That was someone she could talk to, persuade.

He might be some nightmare from the depths, but he was still a person. And people had needs.

They were interrupted by footsteps at the door. Cord stepped in wearing the breastplate, which she'd apparently managed to power. Indeed, her fist glowed with gemstones she'd found.

On one hand, she looked somewhat comical wearing only half of the armor. Her exposed head and arms seemed child-sized with the rest of the Plate in place and functioning. Yet her solemn expression, the way she slammed the butt of a spear down beside her . . . Rysn found herself bolstered by the young woman's determination.

Cord said something loudly in her own language.

"We may speak in Veden," Nikli said, "so Rysn may understand."

"Very well," Cord said. "I challenge you! You must duel me now to the death!"

"I think you'll find I cannot be defeated by a

mortal," Nikli said. "You don't know what you're asking."

"Is that a yes?" Cord bellowed.

"If you insist."

"Ha!" she said. "You have been tricked, god! I am Hualinam'lunanaki'akilu, the daughter of Numuhu-kumakiaki'aialunamor, the Fal'ala'liki'nor, he who drew the Bow of Hours at the dawn of the new millennium, heralding the years of change! If you were to kill me, you would be violating the ancient pact of the Seven Peaks, and so must now forfeit the battle!"

Nikli blinked in what seemed like a very human show of utter confusion. "I . . . have *no idea* what any of that means," he said.

". . . You don't?" Cord asked.

"No."

"Excuse me." She hurried over to Rysn, each footstep clanking on the stone. She knelt. "Are you well?"

"Well as I can be," Rysn said. "Cord . . . I think they're going to kill everyone to keep their secret."

"They don't seem to know about the ancient treaties," Cord whispered. "And in truth, those treaties were made with other gods. I had hoped the Gods Who Sleep Not would be similarly bound, but now I am not certain." She looked down. "I am no warrior, Rysn. I wish to be one, and have claimed this Plate, but I haven't trained to fight. I don't know if these gods can even *be* fought. In the stories, you must always trick them."

"I would rather," Rysn said, her voice loud enough for Nikli to hear, "simply reach an agreement. Surely they can be persuaded."

"Perhaps," Cord said. "The Gods Who Sleep Not are guardians of life. They seek to prevent its end. Use that."

Rysn studied Nikli. He and the others could have killed her by now. But they waited; they *were* willing to talk. They said there was no solution. But if that were the case, why was she still alive?

"Is Cord right?" Rysn said. "Are you protectors of life?"

"We . . ." Nikli said. "We have seen the end of worlds, and vowed never to let such an awful event happen again. But we will kill the few to protect the many, if we must."

"What if I could provide you with another option that didn't involve murdering any more people?"

"We tried," Nikli said. "We did everything we *could* to frighten you away." His skin split along the seams, as if in agitation. "The storm has protected this place for centuries. It is only recently that it weakened enough to let people through. But . . . we are committed, Rysn. By now we've killed hundreds."

"And you've never wondered whether your method is flawed? Yes, you could create *another* fabrication. But will it work? Or will more of the truth seep out? Will you end up with people *swarming* this island? Coming ever closer to the *real* secrets? The ones you hide in these caves?

"You say you wish to protect life. But if you continue on your current course, you're going to have to kill Cord and me. You are going to kill Knights Radiant. If you *truly* are sorry you have to take such desperate actions, don't you owe it to yourself—and the cosmere—to sit and at least *see* if there is another way?"

She turned her hands up, again signaling her desire to begin a deal.

Nikli glanced at his two companions. One barely made an effort to appear human; her skin split at wide seams, and cremlings crawled up and down her body. Neither gave a response Rysn could understand, though the unnerving buzzing surrounding them grew louder.

Finally, Nikli stepped forward and—to Rysn's immense relief—sat at the table.

Lopen managed—barely—to roll out of the way of the arm that speared down at him. But his foot *screamed* in pain and flopped awkwardly on the end of his leg, causing him to see stars and blink away tears. So many painspren crawled around him that he could have started a storming parade.

"Please, gods of the ancient Herdazians," Lopen whispered. "Don't let me get killed by a monster that looks so stupid. *Please*."

The sailors shouted, throwing spears that bounced off the creature, trying to distract it from him. Lopen attempted to push himself up onto one leg to maybe hop away, but it was way too painful. He could barely crawl. And storms, he didn't know *any* one-legged Herdazian jokes.

He flopped to the stones as the thing roared and turned fully toward him. Somehow it knew that a Radiant was a better feast than those sailors. Either that or it was captivated by Lopen's majesty. His lying-on-the-ground-crying-his-eyes-out-all-bloody majesty. So maybe not.

Rua tried to urge Lopen on by taking the shape of an axehound. He bounced around, worried. Huio dropped out of the sky directly in front of Lopen, spear in hand, but his glow faded. Had the things drained him too, or had he run out normally?

Lopen waved for him to go, to run for it with the sailors. But he stayed firm. Stupid chull-brain—he stepped squarely between the monster and Lopen. As it reared to swing, Huio looked right at Lopen, then turned toward the oncoming spear-leg and set himself.

"Huio!" Lopen cried.

His cousin *exploded* with light. A blast of something frigid washed over Lopen, and he found himself disturbing a large frost pattern on the ground in the shape of a glyph.

As the creature's arm reached Huio, mist appeared in the man's hand—forming the biggest, most awesome Shardhammer Lopen had ever seen. Huio slammed it with all his might against the monster's arm, and the carapace cracked and split, spraying violet goo across the stones.

Nikli winced.

"What?" Rysn asked.

"Your friends fight very well," he said.

"They're still alive? You haven't killed them?"

"We have the captain and the crew on the ship held captive," Nikli said. "I persuaded the others to wait to put them down until I'd spoken to you." He held out his hands. "How does this usually proceed?"

"I am the one initiating the trade," Rysn said. "So it is upon me to make an offer."

"You have nothing that we want."

"You want to find a way to avoid killing," Rysn said, keeping her voice steady. "I can help you."

"Wrong," Nikli said. "We wish to avoid losing control of a force that could destroy the cosmere. *That* is what we want, though we do desire to accomplish it with as little suffering as is reasonable."

"Then I can help you," Rysn said. "You want to create a fabrication that others will believe? I will be far better at that than you would be. Both Queen Navani and the Thaylen council will respond better to me telling them that Akinah was a trap than they would to someone like you."

"Except that requires me to trust you with a secret too dangerous to let escape," Nikli said. "Besides, the crew that remains on the ship saw my kind. The sailors will have to die, even if we come up with an accommodation between us."

"No," Rysn said.

"You have no position from which to—"

"I will *not* give up the lives of the captain or any of my crew. That is not negotiable. They are my responsibility."

Nikli lifted his hands to the sides as if to say, "I told you there was no accommodation to be made." It was unnerving how—in the gesture—each of his fingers came free a little, revealing the insectile legs beneath.

Rysn couldn't help staring. "What . . . what are

you?" she found herself whispering, though she probably should have stayed on task.

"I am like you," Nikli said. "Your body is made up of tiny individual pieces called cells. My body is made up of pieces as well."

"Cremlings," she said.

"As I and my kind are not native to this planet, we prefer the term 'hordelings.'"

"And one of them is your brain?" she asked.

"Many of them. We store memories in specialized hordelings bred for the purpose. Cognitive facilities are shared across many different members of the swarm."

He waved his fingers, and again the different little cremlings—no, hordelings—separated. "It took my people three hundred years of selective breeding to achieve hordelings capable of imitating human fingers. And still, most of us are terrible at pretending to be humans. We don't have the mannerisms, the thoughts.

"I'm younger than the others, but am more . . . skilled at using these things." He regarded her. "I have come to understand humans a little, Rysn. I like talking to you, being with you. Though I love your kind, even I am persuaded as to what must be done. Our impasse cannot be resolved."

"No," Rysn said. "There *is* a way." She forcibly made herself use the careful, reasonable tone her babsk had drilled into her. "You say that the sailors have seen you—this can work to our advantage. The best fabrications are mostly true, and having many witnesses corroborate what I say will help."

Nikli shook his head. "Rysn, there are forces in the cosmere that we can barely identify, let alone track. Evil forces, who would end worlds if they could. They are hunting this place. Now that the Ancient Guardians of Akinah are all but extinct, *we* Sleepless must protect it. For if our enemies locate it, they could cause the deaths of billions." He waved toward the mural. "The Dawnshard is . . ."

He stopped. Then he squinted. Then he leaped to his feet. Winged hordelings crawled out of his skull and flew through the air to land on the mural. They scrambled across it, and were joined by hordelings sent by the other two.

"What have you done?" Nikli bellowed. It was unnerving to watch him speak with his head split in two, one of his eyes crawling across the side of his face. "What *have you done*?"

"I— All I did was look at it and—"

Nikli moved suddenly, all conversation abandoned. He reached across the table and grabbed Rysn by the front of her vest. Cord cried out and tried to strike at him, but his body split into pieces before the blow and individual hordelings began crawling up her arms, into her armor.

Others swarmed over Rysn as the man became the monster. He was going to kill her. She didn't know what she'd done, but it clearly meant the end of the negotiations and the beginning of her execution.

In the midst of this, a low, rumbling *roar* shook the cavern.

19

Lopen was so stunned by Huio's transformation,
he was able to ignore the pain for a short time.

Huio. Huio had *beaten* him to the Third Ideal?

Storm it! Rua was cheering, and . . . well, Lopen
was happy for Huio and his spren too. But storm it!
His cousin didn't even have the decency to look embarrassed as he dodged the next leg, then hefted his
Shardhammer—which obligingly became a spear—
and hurled it. It flew straight and true, like a silvery
line of light, and struck the creature in the head. Not
in the eye, but with a Shardweapon that didn't matter so much. It went right through the thick carapace
and sliced out the other side.

The giant grublike monster teetered, then col-
lapsed with a cracking sound that reminded Lopen

how hungry he was. Nothing like crab legs after a hard day of being beaten up.

Huio puffed in and out, then stared at his hands in awe as his Shardhammer re-formed. He turned with a stupid grin on his face. Then he rushed over to help Lopen sit up.

That gave both of them a great view of the bay, which started to bubble and churn. *Six* more of those monsters began to rise.

"Damnation," Huio muttered. "You have any more Stormlight, cousin?"

"No. You?"

"No. I got a burst when I said the Ideal, but that ran out fast."

"I see," Lopen said. "Tell me. What are your thoughts on, say, carrying your wonderful cousin on your back as you run for safety?"

The roar was so loud that chips fell from the ceiling of the chamber. The hordelings swarming over Rysn and Cord stopped. Nikli had only a semblance of humanity left, his face and chest split open, skin hanging from the backs of the various pieces with twitching legs, his insides squirming and buzzing. But many of the hordelings turned toward the sound.

The door to the side blew open farther, revealing

the larger hall with the skulls of dead greatshells. Rysn could have *sworn* that they'd turned to stare in toward the smaller chamber. Six of them lined the hall, which narrowed as it extended, letting each set of dead eyes look past the ones in front.

Rysn felt something fluttering around her. Glowing white arrowhead spren, moving like fish in an unseen stream, swirling around her and Cord. That roar reverberated in her ears, in her memory. It didn't repeat, but a higher-pitched squeal echoed in the hallway. And then a small figure leaped up and landed on top of one of the skulls, flapping her wings and letting out a mighty—yet diminutive—roar.

Chiri-Chiri had returned. Surely she hadn't made that other roar, the one that had vibrated Rysn to the core. Yet Chiri-Chiri gave it her best, calling out again. She seemed . . . rather tiny atop the big skull, like a child with a wooden sword standing in a line of fully armored knights. Still, she hopped off the carapace skull and came loping across the stones, roaring and buzzing her wings to fly at the top of each leap. She yelled her little heart out, as angry as Rysn had ever seen her.

The larkin bounded over to Rysn and hopped onto the table, then trumped with all her might at the three Sleepless. Nikli's hordelings withdrew into his body, forming the semblance of a human again.

Chiri-Chiri looked much better. The chalky white cast to her carapace had vanished, her natural violet-brown colors returning. She wasn't terribly fearsome, considering her size, but she did her best, bless her. She stood between Rysn and Nikli. Growling, snapping, and howling in challenge.

"Ancient Guardian," Nikli said to Chiri-Chiri—still speaking Veden—standing up on the other side of the table. "We should have realized you would find your way to this chamber, but you are no longer needed to protect the secret. At the fall of your kind, mine took up the mantle."

"The secret," Rysn said, "that has . . . somehow entered my brain."

"That will soon be fixed," Nikli said.

"These creatures . . ." Cord said. "They protected this place once, you said?" She shivered, and Rysn couldn't blame her, after feeling those strange insects on her skin. Cord glanced down the hallway at the skulls, then back at Chiri-Chiri. "She's one of them. She returned to protect the treasure."

"Coincidence!" Nikli said. "Chiri-Chiri simply reached the size where she needed to bond a mandra to continue growing."

"Others of her kind don't grow at all," Rysn said. "Chiri-Chiri did. She brought me here."

"The spren guided us," Cord said. "This thing was the gods' will."

"The force inside my mind asked me to choose," Rysn said. "It wanted me to accept it, whatever it is."

"No it did not!" Nikli said. "The Dawnshard isn't alive. It doesn't *want* things. You have stolen it!"

And Rysn knew, or at least felt, he was partially right. It wasn't a living thing that she'd taken upon herself. It was . . . something else. A Command. It didn't have a will, and it hadn't led her here or chosen her.

But Chiri-Chiri had done both.

"Do you see them?" Cord asked, gesturing to the roof of the cavern. "Joining us, watching us? Do you see the gods?"

Rysn took a deep breath, then turned her palms upward again. "It appears," she said, "that I *do* have something you want. Shall we continue the negotiations?"

"You are a thief!" Nikli said, his body dropping hordelings as he stepped toward Rysn. "You cannot bargain with stolen goods!"

He reached for Rysn, but Chiri-Chiri reared up and let out another shout. This one was different somehow. Not a tantrum, not just a warning. An ultimatum. Something about the way it resonated in the room made Nikli hesitate.

Think, Rysn. You need to give him something. Many traders tried to sell people a "bargain" they did not want, but that was not the path to a sustainable partnership. You had to give them something they actually needed.

Nikli stepped forward again. Chiri-Chiri growled.

"Do not assume we would not kill an Ancient Guardian if we had to," Nikli said to her.

"You claim to want to protect this thing," Rysn said, "but all you threaten to do is destroy."

"If you knew what the Dawnshard was capable of . . ."

"It's now inside me. Whatever it is."

"Fortunately, you would not be able to employ it," Nikli said. "It is beyond your capacity. But there are those in the cosmere who could use it for terrible acts."

Rysn glanced at the other two, noting how *distressed* their hordelings seemed. She heard uncertainty in Nikli's voice now. And for the first time, she saw them as they truly were.

Terrified.

They were unraveling. They were failing. They clung to a secret that was escaping despite their best efforts. As Vstim had taught her, she saw through *their* eyes. Felt their fears, their loss, their uncertainty.

"How far you have fallen," she whispered. "You would murder the very guardians you revere? You would rip the Dawnshard forcibly from the mind of the one who bears it? *You* would *become* the things you pretend to defend against."

Nikli slumped to the ground. His skin split, making him look like a husk.

Don't give them what they say they want, she thought. *Give them what they need.*

"You say you fight hidden enemies you cannot locate," Rysn said. "They could use this thing, but I cannot. It seems to me that the safest place for it is in my mind."

"How?" Nikli demanded.

"Your secret is escaping, Nikli. You know you can't hold it in. The storm ever blows, and the walls crack. You furiously plug the leaks, but the entire structure is collapsing. Your lies undermine one another.

"They *will* come. The ones you fear. How valuable would it be for you to be able to watch and see who they are? What if you could trap *them*, instead of innocent crews of sailors?"

"Innocent?" Nikli asked. "You came for loot."

"Salvage," Rysn said. "It sounds more civilized.

Plus, you know that was only a small part of our quest here."

Nikli thought. "It is too dangerous," he said. "If our enemies came here, they'd find our secret."

"Unless it wasn't here," Rysn said. "Unless it was somewhere completely unexpected—like in the mind of a random human woman. Who would assume you'd let one leave with something so powerful?

"Nikli, too many people, when they get something valuable, sit on it and sit on it—anticipating the trade they will someday make. They imagine how grand it will be! How much they will earn! In the meantime, they eat scraps. Do you know how many die with that nest egg, never spent, never used?

"What you want—the safeguarding of this mystery—is possible, but you need to be active. You need to make a trade, build alliances, and identify your enemies. Sitting here, hoping to simply hold on so tightly . . . it won't work. Trust me, Nikli. Sometimes you *need* to accept what you've lost, then move *forward*. Then you can instead realize what you've gained."

He slumped, but many of the hordelings looked at her. It was unnerving, yet it seemed promising.

"Nikli," Rysn whispered. "Remember what I taught you. About coming to know the sailors. About the hazing. Not a perfect solution . . ."

"But instead an imperfect solution," he whispered, "for an imperfect world." He remained like a husk, but his hordelings started buzzing to the other two swarms.

After a long time of buzzing back and forth, Nikli spoke.

"What would it take," he said, "to make this deal?"

"Not much. I can tell the story exactly as it happened, but leave out that mural. Cord and I swam down here, found the Plate and Soulcasters. You were going to attack us, to protect these treasures, but you were impressed by Chiri-Chiri—one of the Ancient Guardians of this place.

"Her valiance in defending me made you pause. Because of the time we spent together, and because of my persuasive nature, I convinced you that we are not your enemies. You decided to let us go."

"People will hear of the Oathgate. You cannot hide that. Everyone will come to the island."

"Exactly!" Rysn said. "That's what we want. Let the Oathgate be opened, and allow scholars to swarm this place! The enemies you fear? They will drive themselves mad searching the island for the secret that's not here!"

"Because it is in your mind," Nikli said. "Something they'd never believe that we would allow. We, who protect planets, letting this power enter a mortal . . . An imperfect solution, yet perhaps . . ." He met her eyes. "There is a flaw. Your people might believe that we just let you go, but our enemies? They will push to find out the truth."

"So we need another layer," Rysn said, nodding. "A secret for them to 'discover.' We tell everyone that you let us go because you were impressed. Or maybe something a little more . . . mythological. Cord, how would the stories say a meeting like this might play out?"

Cord gave it some thought, then looked up again. "Luckspren. There are legends of them leading to treasure, yes? But there are always guardians of treasure. And in the stories, you complete their challenges, then get a reward."

"So we tell everyone that," Rysn said, "but to our queens and other dignitaries we tell a more subtle lie, one very close to the truth. That I negotiated with you for the treasure—the Shardplate and Soulcasters, saying nothing of the thing in my mind. Those who spy and push for secrets will discover this."

"We would still need a trade," Nikli said, "that is plausible. Something our enemies believe we'd trade to you. Yet my people have few wants. . . ."

"But you do," Rysn said. "You said it earlier. Your kind are bad at pretending to be humans—so our trade is for training. I agree to take some of you with me, and to show you how to be human. We train you."

"That . . ." Nikli said. "That could work. Yes, they'd believe that lie. The Soulcasters are practically useless to my kind. We keep them out of reverence, as they were offerings to the Ancient Guardians long ago. But one is with you, so it makes sense to trade them to you . . . and we do need training. It's something we've often complained about." He glanced toward Cord. "This one will know our secret."

"I am of the Peaks," Cord said. "Guardians of the pool. You know I can be trusted."

Nikli buzzed with the others of his kind, then he looked Cord up and down. "If we agree to this deal, we will trade the Soulcasters to Rysn for training and aid in imitating humans. That armor you wear, however, has long been reserved for guardians of the Dawnshard. If you would bear it, you will bear that burden as well."

"I . . . will ponder this task," Cord said. "I have many loyalties that come before this thing."

"If we are going to accept—and I cannot promise we will, as all the Sleepless must vote—this woman *must* be protected. She will need bodyguards!"

"I will have the Dawnshard's larkin guardian," Rysn said. "Who is its true defender, if what you've said to me is true. I would welcome more help, but remember, the point of all this is to *not* hint at what I've done. Too many people watching me would defeat that purpose. I assume your hordelings can monitor me quietly. I wouldn't be able to prevent you, and honestly, I'd rather know you're there."

"Plus," Cord said, "this thing will help with the lie—if your enemies spot you near Rysn, they will think you are training, as per the deal we have made."

"The deal we are *considering*," Nikli said. "It is not agreed. You don't even know what it is you've done, Rysn. You don't understand what it is that is now inside your head."

"So . . . tell me?"

Nikli laughed. "Mere words cannot explain. The Dawnshards are Commands, Rysn. The will of a god."

"I feel what you say is right, but . . . I had always imagined the Dawnshards as weapons, like the mythical Honorblades." To be honest, she'd rarely heard the term "Dawnshard," but she was pretty sure she'd always conflated them with Honorblades.

"The most powerful forms of Surgebinding transcend traditional mortal understanding," Nikli said. His body began to re-form, hordelings crawling back into place. "All their greatest applications require *Intent* and a *Command*. Demands on a level no person could ever manage alone. To make such Commands, one must have the reasoning—the breadth of understanding—of a deity. And so, the Dawn-shards. The four primal *Commands* that created all things." He paused. "And then eventually, they were used to undo Adonalsium itself. . . ."

Cord whispered something in her own language.

"So you *do* know," Nikli said to her.

"There are songs . . ." Cord said. "From long ago. Of when this . . . Command came through the pool." She whispered again in her tongue, and it sounded like a prayer.

Rysn was watching several hordelings that had slipped around near her. These looked strikingly like Chiri-Chiri in miniature.

"We once assumed," Nikli said, noticing her attention, "that the last of the lanceryn had died, and the few hordelings we had bred with them were all that remained. Inferior bloodlines, though they give us the ability to negate some applications of Stormlight. Yours is the third larkin we now know to have survived—but the only one that has grown mature enough to return here."

Chiri-Chiri had settled down on the table, though she watched the three Sleepless and clicked warningly.

"Why . . . did you say she needed to return?" Rysn asked. "Will she grow sick again?"

"Larger greatshells need to bond mandras—you call them luckspren—to keep from crushing themselves to death with their own weight. The mandras of this place are special. Smaller, yet more potent, than the common breeds. It is no simple thing to make a creature as heavy as a lancer—or larkin, as they are now called—fly. Chiri-Chiri will need to return every few years until she is fully grown."

"Fully grown?" Rysn said, turning again toward those skulls. "Oh storms . . ."

"You should never have come here," Nikli said. "You should have been dissuaded. But . . . we cannot deny that what you said is true. You *were* brought by the needs of an Ancient Guardian. And unfortunately, the rest of what you say is also true. Our secret leaks into the world. This Dawnshard is no longer safe. I must say . . . I had not anticipated being persuaded in this matter."

"It is the job of a trademaster to see a need, then fulfill it," Rysn said. She felt the strange pressure in the back of her mind. It was a Command? How had it been *in* the mural, but now invaded her head? She hadn't been able to read the writing. What kind of Command wasn't written, but *infused* a subject like Stormlight in a sphere?

Nikli stood up, his hordelings snapping together. He pulled his robe tight. "We will discuss." Behind, the other two disintegrated completely, turning into piles. "Then we will vote. It will not take long, as the others have been relaying our conversation to all the swarms. We communicate faster than humans."

"Nikli," Rysn said. "When you speak to them, I have a request. Among my people, during important treaty negotiations, both parties often bring a witness of integrity. Someone to speak to the moral character of the diplomats involved. Tell me, are you the same person who has traveled with me these months? You didn't somehow replace the real Nikli?"

"I am the same person you hired," Nikli said. "My initial task was to watch the Ancient Guardian and assess whether she was being cared for. Beyond that, we had a reasonable guess that an expedition would soon come here via a Thaylen ship. And yours is the finest of the fleet. It was a simple decision to place me in the crew of the *Wandersail*."

"Then you've sailed with me," Rysn said. "You know me. When you speak to the others, I want you to tell them—honestly—what you think of me."

"I don't know if—"

"All I ask is honesty," Rysn said. "Tell them about me, and what kind of trademaster I am."

He nodded, then broke into hordelings—like a person who had frozen in cold Southern winds, then shattered.

Cord knelt beside her. "You did well," she whispered. "As well as anyone in the songs, when dealing with dangerous gods. But you did not trick him."

"Hopefully this is better," Rysn whispered back.

Cord nodded, but then immediately began working on the Plate to get the last pieces powered. She plainly wanted to be ready, just in case.

It wouldn't be enough. Rysn waited, tense, watching the hordelings chitter and move, as if the many pieces were at least slightly autonomous. Nikli had said his conference with the others would not take long, but Rysn found the wait almost unbearable.

After about five minutes, Nikli re-formed. "It is done."

"And . . . how did it go?" Rysn asked.

"They . . . listened. The others think this is a promising idea you propose, and appreciate the dual nature of the lies, layered to trick our enemies. My kin insisted on two further terms, though. You must *never* bond a spren to become a Radiant."

"I . . . doubt Chiri-Chiri would be willing to share me," she said. "I hadn't considered it, not seriously."

"Also, you may not tell anyone what has happened to you," Nikli said. "Unless you ask us first. I . . . explained to them that humans often need people to confide in. They pointed to Cord as one, but I suggested we might need more. If we are going to maintain this secret, and work with humans to protect the Dawnshard, there could be others we need. You will speak to us before you do these things, and you may only tell them what we agree to let you."

"I agree to these terms," Rysn said, "so long as you promise that none of my crew are to be harmed by your kind. They are . . . still alive, aren't they?"

"Regrettably, there has been a conflict on the beach with some of our more . . . specialized hordelings," Nikli said. "The Radiants have led the crew to the city to hide, and I believe three of the sailors have died. Those on the ship have been kept safe, per my request."

Rysn felt a twist in her stomach for those she'd failed. At the same time, she had worried that far more had died. This was much better than she'd feared.

"And you," Nikli said to Cord. "You will protect the Dawnshard, fight for its defense?"

"No," Cord said, standing up, helm under her arm.

"But—" Nikli began.

"I am no soldier," Cord said, her voice growing softer. "I am no warrior. I must train if I am to be of any use. I will go to war and learn to use this gift. I will fight the Void, as my father refuses to do. Once I've accomplished that goal, then I will consider your request."

Nikli glanced toward Rysn, who shrugged. "I mean . . . she has a point, Nikli."

"Fine," Nikli said, with a very human sigh. "But Cord, you will vow upon the honor of both your mother and your father that you will bear this secret and tell no one. Not even blood relatives."

"I had not thought you knew my people that well," Cord said. "I will take this vow." She then spoke it in her own tongue.

"Our accommodation is reached?" Rysn asked, hopeful.

"Yes," he said. "There will be smaller details to arrange at a later date. But we give our agreement to your terms, Rysn Ftori bah-Vstim. Your life for being honorable. These Soulcasters and Plate for the promise to train and help us."

She felt an overwhelming sense of relief. Never, when listening to Vstim's lessons, had she imagined she might one day need them to bargain for her life. And perhaps more.

"So, Rysn is a Shardbearer now?" Cord asked. "A . . . Dawnshardbearer?"

"No," Nikli said. "She bears nothing. She *is* the Dawnshard now. That is how it works." He bowed to Rysn. "We will speak again."

Rysn braced herself on the bench, then bowed back.

Storms, she thought. *What have I done?*

What you needed to, another part of her thought. *You have adapted. You have Remade yourself.*

It was then that she grasped, in the smallest way, the nature of the Command inside her. The will of a god to remake things, to demand they be better.

The power to change.

EPILOGUE

Lopen patted the rocks fondly. "I will never forget you," he said to them. "Or the time we shared together."

Rushu tucked away her notepad, apparently having finished her final sketch of the broken city. They were doing one last round of the place, some hours after the battle.

"It was a brave thing you did," Lopen said to the rocks. "Though I know you are only rocks and cannot listen to me—because you are dead, or really were never alive—you must hear that I appreciate your sacrifice."

"Could you be . . . less weird maybe?" Rushu asked. "For a day at least. To try it out? Experience the world the way the rest of us do?"

"You saw what these rocks did."

"I saw one of the monsters trip," Rushu said, "if that's what you mean."

They'd made it all the way to the city ruins—Lopen on Huio's back—before the monsters had caught up to them. He remembered huddling in one of the fallen buildings—Rushu had scouted a location for them that had a roof—waiting for the end to come. And then one of the monsters had stumbled.

Of course, sure, five minutes later the things had all turned around and returned to the ocean. Lopen hadn't known it at the time, but this was because Brightness Rysn had negotiated peace. Still, that time the monster had tripped on the rocks had bought at least ten seconds.

"Didn't your cousin *literally* save your life?" Rushu said, joining Lopen as they walked to the beach.

"Yeah, he did," Lopen said.

Thanking Huio was going to be harder than thanking a bunch of rocks. So Lopen had wanted to practice.

At the beach, Kstled waited with two rowboats to take them to the *Wandersail*. They'd somehow transitioned from near death to leaving with a ridiculous haul. Shardplate, a mountain of gemstones—real this time—and some Soulcasters?

"Remind me never to cross Brightness Rysn,"

Lopen said. "I don't know what those challenges are she passed, but I can't believe it ended with us so rich. And so, well, alive."

"Yes, I agree," Rushu said. "There *is* something strange about all this, isn't there?" She tapped her pen against her lips, then shook her head and walked down to climb into a boat. They were leaving for Thaylenah—they'd been offered the chance to stay, now that the mysterious trials were done, but nobody wanted to hang around. Why tempt fate?

At the beach, Lopen nodded to Kstled, who got into the boat with Rushu, leaving Lopen and Huio alone in the other one. Huio seemed surprised by this, but Lopen had arranged it. He settled into the seat and began rowing. Wasn't too difficult, so long as you had two arms.

"Can't believe we're getting away," Huio said, watching the island retreat. "What do you suppose happened in that cavern underneath?"

"None of our business, I think," Lopen said.

Huio grunted. "Wise words, younger-cousin. Sure. Wise words."

They sat quietly for a time, Lopen navigating the boat toward the *Wandersail*. "So," Lopen finally said. "Third Ideal, eh? Congratulations, older-cousin."

"Thanks."

"That's . . . the ideal where you agree to protect people you hate. Least it was for Kaladin, Teft, and Sig."

"Yeah," Huio said.

"And you looked right at me," Lopen said softly, "before you achieved it."

"Doesn't have to mean what you think," Huio said. "You heard Teft tell us about his oath. For him, it meant coming to realize he couldn't keep hating himself."

"Was it the same for you, then?" Lopen asked, slowly pulling the oars. One stroke after another. When Huio didn't respond, he continued more softly, "It's okay, Huio. I can hear it. I need to."

"I don't hate you, Lopen," Huio said. "Who could hate you? It would take a special kind of bitter soul."

"That statement, like the Lopen himself, sounds like it comes with a quite spectacular butt attached."

Huio smiled, then leaned forward. He was so often solemn, Lopen's older-cousin. Built like a boulder and kind of resembling one, with that balding head. Everyone misunderstood Huio. Maybe even the Lopen himself.

"I *don't* hate you," Huio said. "But you *can* be a pain, younger-cousin. Me, Punio, Fleeta, even Mama Lond. The way you joke can sometimes hurt us."

"I joke with the people I love. It's how I am."

"Yes, but does it *have* to be?" Huio asked. "Could you, sure, tease a little less?"

"I . . ."

Storms. Was it true? Was that how they thought of him? Lopen pasted a smile on and nodded to Huio, who seemed relieved that the conversation had gone so well.

They reached the ship, and Rua hovered about Lopen's head as he laughed with the sailors he met—but he slowly made his way to the small cabin he shared with Huio. For now, Huio gave him space to go in. Sit down. And stare.

"Do . . . others complain about me?" Lopen asked Rua, who settled onto the table. "Do my jokes . . . actually hurt people?"

The little spren shrugged. Then nodded. Sometimes they did.

"Stormfather," Lopen whispered. "I just want people to be happy. That's what I try to do. Make them smile."

Rua nodded again, solemn.

Lopen felt a sudden sharp pain in his breast, accompanied by shamespren sprinkling around him like red flower petals. It threatened to spread, to encompass him. It made him want to curl up and never say another word. Maybe they'd like that. A quiet Lopen.

Storm it, he thought. *No. No, I gotta take this like Bridge Four. Arrow straight to the heart, but I can pull it out and heal.* Huio could have held the truth back, laughed everything off. But he'd trusted Lopen with this wound.

"I'll do it, then," Lopen said, standing up. "I've got to protect people, you know? Even from myself. Gotta rededicate to being the best Lopen possible. A better, improved, *extra*-incredible Lopen."

Rua lifted his hand into the air in a fist. Then the little spren toppled over to the side.

"Rua?" Lopen said, leaning down. "You playing a trick on me, naco?"

Rua vanished. Then a silvery little dagger appeared in his place. What on Roshar? Lopen picked it up. It was physical, not insubstantial. It was . . .

THESE WORDS ARE ACCEPTED.

A burst of frost and power exploded around Lopen.

"Storm me!" Lopen shouted, looking at the ceiling. "You did it *again*? I almost died out there, and you accept the Words *now*?"

IT IS THE RIGHT TIME.

"Where's the drama?" Lopen demanded at the sky. "The sense of timing? You're *terrible* at this, penhito!"

I TAKE OFFENSE AT THAT. BE GLAD FOR WHAT YOU HAVE.

"I didn't even know I'd said it!" Lopen muttered.

Storm it. Stupid oath. But he tried out the dagger, and it changed to a nice silvery sword, beautiful and ornate. He'd expected a little engraving of Rua making a rude gesture. And of course as he thought about it, that exact thing appeared on the blade. Huh.

This offered a *ton* of possibilities. . . .

No, no. He would be better. No pranks. Or, well, fewer pranks. He could do that. Protect people from himself. Who'd ever heard of an oath like that?

But, well, he *was* the Lopen. Things *should* be different for him. "Hey Huio!" he shouted, yanking open the door. "You're *never* going to guess what just happened!"

R ysn didn't let herself relax until the winds finally stopped blowing and calm sunlight streamed in through the porthole of her cabin. The ship was free of the storm around Akinah.

They had actually been allowed to leave.

Not that she was alone. A few hordelings accompanied her in secret. Representatives of the Sleepless, who would train with her and keep watch over her. Likely for the rest of her life.

But the arrangement had been made, the details hammered out. The lie was the best kind, as it required very little actual lying. Almost all of what they had to say was true, and of the crew, only Rysn and Cord knew the full secret.

Chiri-Chiri chirped nearby from a set of towels she'd arranged into a nest. She looked so content now, full of color. She'd spent the ride bouncing around and prancing through the room, then flying near the ceiling. As full of energy as Rysn had ever seen her.

Would Chiri-Chiri retain the ability to fly as she grew big as a chasmfiend? Nikli had implied she would. Stormwinds. How would Rysn deal with that? How long would it take?

Well, she'd handle it when the time came. She was less confident about the other burden, the one in her mind. She'd spent this entire voyage wondering if she belonged here, in this seat. And now she'd entered territory no babsk could ever have trained her to traverse.

But she'd certainly had lots of practice sitting up straight these last years. And in a way, she found that she felt *comforted*. If no one had traveled this path before, then she didn't have to compare herself to anyone, did she? She didn't have to be Vstim. Not in this task.

"Is that why you chose me?" Rysn asked Chiri-Chiri. "Did you know I could bear this?"

The larkin chirped encouragingly. And it was incredible how much better that made her feel. Rysn used her arms to scoot her body along the bench and poured some tea. At last she felt relaxed enough to read through the responses from the monarchs. Mostly confirmations of what she'd sent. They would want to speak to her in person to get the details. There, she would confide in them the second half-lie. That she had agreed to train the Sleepless.

Storms. Was it her, or did this tea taste extra good? She inspected it, then glanced at the sunlight pouring through the porthole. Was it ... brighter than usual? Why did the colors in her room look so exceptionally vivid all of a sudden?

A knock came at her door.

"Come in," she said, taking another sip of the wonderful tea.

Captain Drlwan entered, then bowed. Outside, Cord continued her vigil of guarding Rysn's door—wearing full Shardplate. "You're really going to let her keep it?" Drlwan said softly as she came up from her bow.

"Cord discovered it," Rysn said. "It's traditional to let the one who first claims a Shard keep it." The Command pulsed with warmth as she said that. "Besides, Cord saved my life."

"The Alethi won't be happy," Drlwan said. "They have a history of laying dubious—but strongly enforced—claim to Shards."

"They'll deal with the pain of losing this one," Rysn said. "They're getting three Soulcasters, after all."

Drlwan smiled at that. Five of the new Soulcasters would go to Thaylenah. For years the Alethi had possessed a near monopoly on food-creating Soulcasters, but Thaylenah would now possess two—along with one that could form metals, one that created smoke, and another focused on wood, matching the one that the city had used for ages to make the best seafaring lumber.

A true wealth that would benefit Thaylenah for generations. And with the gemstones found in the caverns, the crew would have their promised riches, in compensation for the danger they'd undertaken.

She still mourned the three men she'd lost. It seemed such a waste of their lives when an agreement had been reached so soon after. She wondered if generals ever grieved for the last people who died before a treaty was signed.

Captain Drlwan settled down in the seat beside the desk. She didn't speak for a long moment, instead looking past Rysn at the sunlight streaming in through the porthole.

"I didn't think we'd see the sun again," Drlwan finally said. "Not once those . . . things arrived. Even after you returned, I expected them to make some beast sink the *Wandersail* as it was leaving, then blame it on the storm."

"I'll admit," Rysn said, "those same fears occurred to me."

"What *are* they, Rysn?" the captain asked. "Truly? They seem like monsters of nightmare and the Void."

"Most people who are different from us are frightening at first," Rysn said. "But one thing Vstim taught me was to see past my own expectations. In this case, it meant looking past what I assumed made someone a person, and seeing the humanity—and the fear—in what appeared to be a nightmare."

"They told me," the captain said, "what you did."

Rysn felt a spike of alarm, cup held halfway to her lips. What? They'd talked about the Dawnshard, after all this?

"As the ones on the ship were leaving," Drlwan said. "Before you returned. They told me you had a chance to bargain for your own life. They said you would not enter into a negotiation unless it included the safety of the entire crew."

Ah. That part. Rysn's anxiety faded. "I did what any rebsk would do."

"Pardon," the captain said. "But you did what any *good* rebsk would do. A rebsk worthy of this crew."

They shared a look, then Rysn nodded her thanks.

"After we leave port on our third journey," Drlwan said, standing, "it would be good for the crew to see you steer the ship for a short time, would it not?"

"I would be honored," Rysn said, her voice catching as she said it. "Truly."

Drlwan smiled. "Let us hope the next one is a more . . . traditional voyage."

Rysn's eyes flicked to a purple hordeling hiding on the wall, near where it met the ceiling, shadowed. Strange, how she saw the contrast of shadows much more starkly now. And . . . why did Drlwan's voice sound more musical?

"I think," Rysn said, "I shall select the most boring, most mundane trade expedition I can find, Captain."

That satisfied Drlwan. Rysn settled back—a single gloryspren fading overhead—and thought upon those words. *Mundane. Boring.* She had an inkling that neither would ever accurately describe her life again.

ACKNOWLEDGMENTS

I feel especially appreciative with this book, which was supported by the community directly. For those who don't know, this book was initially produced as a result of a successful Kickstarter campaign for *The Way of Kings* leatherbound. So the first acknowledgment is to all of you! Thank you for your active enthusiasm for this series, which I always thought would be too strange and too enormous to be popular.

Putting *Dawnshard* together at the speed we did required a lot of work and time from many people. At their forefront is the indefatigable Peter Ahlstrom, editorial director at my company and primary editor of this volume. In addition, Karen Ahlstrom—continuity editor—did a lot of great work helping with the intricacies of this book's timeline. Kristina Kugler was our line editor on this book, and she was fantastic as always. The team at Tor who worked on this book includes Greg Collins, Rafal Gibek, Jim Kapp, Molly McGhee, and Devi Pillai.

The cover illustration and design were done by Ben McSweeney and Isaac Stewart, with Isaac Stewart acting as art director and Ben providing the illustrations—including the icons at the heads of chapters.

The writing group for this book was Kaylynn ZoBell, Ben Oldsen, Alan Layton, Ethan Skarstedt, Kathleen Dorsey Sanderson, Eric James Stone, Darci Stone, Peter Ahlstrom, and Karen Ahlstrom.

Of special note for this book, we had a group of accessibility and paraplegia experts who gave me a ton of great feedback—leading to not just a better book in their specific area of expertise, but a more engaging and interesting book overall. They include Eliza Stauffer, Chana Oshira Block, Whitney Sivill, Sam Lytal, and Toby Cole.

Our beta reader team included Alice Arneson, Richard Fife, Darci Cole, Christina Goodman, Deana Whitney, Ravi Persaud, Paige Vest, Trae Cooper, Drew McCaffrey, Bao Pham, Lyndsey "Lyn" Luther, Eric Lake, Brian T. Hill, Nikki Ramsay, Paige Phillips, Leah Zine, Sam Lytal, Jessica Ashcraft, Ian McNatt, Mark Lindberg, Jessie Bell, David Behrens, Whitney Sivill, Chana Oshira Block, Nathan Goodrich, Marnie Peterson, Eliza Stauffer, and Toby Cole.

Gamma readers included many of the beta readers plus: Bao Pham, Aaron Ford, Frankie Jerome,

Shannon Nelson, Linnea Lindstrom, Sam Baskin, Ross Newberry, Evgeni "Argent" Kirilov, Jennifer Neal, Tim Challener, Ted Herman, Chris McGrath, Glen Vogelaar, Poonam Desai, Todd H. Singer, Suzanne Musin, Gary Singer, Christopher Cottingham, Joshua Harkey, and Lingting "Botanica" Xu.

It should be noted that many of them, after just having finished the beta/gamma for *Rhythm of War*, went right into this book in order to get it done on time. I sincerely appreciate their wisdom, thoughtful feedback, and effort.

ABOUT THE AUTHOR

Brandon Sanderson grew up in Lincoln, Nebraska. He lives in Utah with his wife and children and teaches creative writing at Brigham Young University. He is the author of such bestsellers as the Mistborn® saga, *Warbreaker*, The Stormlight Archive® series beginning with *The Way of Kings*, *The Rithmatist*, the Skyward series, the Reckoners® series beginning with *Steelheart*, and the Alcatraz vs. the Evil Librarians series. He won the 2013 Hugo Award for *The Emperor's Soul*, a novella set in the world of his acclaimed first novel, *Elantris*. Additionally, he was chosen to complete Robert Jordan's The Wheel of Time®. For behind-the-scenes information on all of Brandon Sanderson's books, visit brandonsanderson.com.